THE LOVE TOKEN

CINDY KIRK

This is a work of fiction. Names, characters, places and incidents are products of the author's imagination or are used fictitiously. Any resemblance to actual events, locales, organizations, or persons, living or dead, is entirely coincidental.

ISBN: 9798841269199

1

"You look positively mah-velous, darling."

Sophia Jessup's lips curved at the compliment. After taking a second to adjust her straw hat, she turned from her reflection in the antique beveled mirror and smiled at the woman in the doorway to Timeless Treasures.

Standing nearly six feet tall, Ruby Osentowski—Sophie's bestie and second-in-command here at the store—was known for her quick wit and eclectic fashion sense.

Today, wearing a midi boho-chic caftan with an ostrich feather imprint, Ruby definitely drew the eye. Reacting to the humidity that was GraceTown, Maryland, in the summer, Ruby's brown hair exploded around her pretty face in a riot of curls.

"What are you doing here already?" Sophie feigned confusion. "You aren't due in for another hour."

"And you're not supposed to be here at all. But I knew I'd find you here. Just like you knew I'd be early." With a smug smile, Ruby strode down the center aisle toward Sophie, passing a display of mechanical coin banks and artfully arranged vintage cereal boxes.

When she reached the back sales counter, Ruby handed

Sophie a cup from Perkatory, a coffee shop down the block, before calling out, "Andrew, I brought coffee."

Andrew Doman, college student and part-time employee for the last year, appeared from the back. Tall with a mop of brown hair, he sported black-rimmed glasses that had a habit of sliding down his nose.

Crossing to them, he picked up the cup Ruby had set on the counter. "Three sugars?"

Ruby winked. "I know what you like."

"Thanks, Ruby." Andrew took a long sip, then jerked a thumb in Sophie's direction. "I tried to tell this one we're capable of handling anything that comes our way today, but she showed up anyway."

"You know I trust both of you implicitly. I'm just here, well, because I want to be." Sophie lifted one shoulder, then let it drop. "Besides, my apartment is just upstairs."

"Excuses, excuses." The smile on Ruby's full lips took any sting out of the words. "Fess up. You wanted to see us."

Sophie rolled her eyes, but knew there was truth in Ruby's offhand comment. She loved spending time with Ruby and Andrew.

"I'm going to take my coffee with me to the back room. We have quite a few items needing sales tags." Andrew shifted his gaze to Ruby and gestured with his hand holding the cup. "Yell if you need me."

Just before he stepped out of sight, Andrew turned and pinned Sophie with a stern gaze, a look spoiled when his glasses slipped down. "Have fun today. That's an order."

Chuckling, Sophie gave a mock salute. "Yes, sir."

Sophie couldn't believe the change in Andrew. When he'd started working for her last year, he'd been oh-so-serious. She liked that he now felt comfortable enough to crack jokes and give her grief.

"Andrew fits right in." Lifting the cup, Sophie took a sip of the mocha latte Ruby had brought her. "Thank you for this. It's yummy."

"You're very welcome." Ruby sat on a stool at the counter and studied Sophie. "I'm glad you decided to take some time off."

"Me, too." Sophie smiled. "Volunteering refills my bucket."

Ruby swiveled on her stool to fully face Sophie. "A Chautauqua is your kind of thing."

"Yes, it is."

Chautauqua, an adult education and social movement popular in the late nineteenth and early twentieth centuries, had recently experienced a resurgence. GraceTown had chosen to re-create performances from 1916 and had encouraged those in the community to attend dressed in period garb.

When Sophie had been asked to volunteer, she'd eagerly accepted and had persuaded her boyfriend, Dylan Connors, to sign up with her.

"You'll have a blast." Ruby's gaze returned to Sophie's blue sailor dress. "That dress is absolutely adorable on you."

"I love it." As Sophie gave a little twirl, she couldn't stop herself from casting one last glance in the mirror. The red necktie, a last-minute addition to the sailor dress, added a nice pop of color. "I can't wait to get to the fairgrounds and see what everyone else is wearing."

Ruby inclined her head. "I didn't realize women wore such cute clothes in 1916. For some reason I had the impression you couldn't show ankles until the 1920s."

"That was how it was in the early 1900s, but by 1916, skirts were on the rise," Sophie assured Ruby.

"Your knowledge of history is only one of the reasons Timeless Treasures is so successful." Ruby glanced at the shiny hardwood floor, then sniffed. "Not only do we have all sorts of fabulous antiques, instead of mold and dust, the place is spotless and smells terrific."

Sophie puffed up with pride.

Five years ago, after purchasing the store in GraceTown's historic district from money bequeathed to her in her grandmother's will, Sophie had gone into research mode, determined to make the store a success.

When she'd come across studies showing that smells not only influenced people's emotions but their spending, she'd begun infusing a simple orange scent into her store. That was only one of many changes she'd implemented.

While her parents worried about all the hours she put in at Timeless Treasures, Sophie loved every aspect of the antique store business.

Though she'd enjoyed her work as an archivist at Collister College, dealing with antiques day in and day out was a dream come true. She couldn't imagine anything better than owning a business that dealt in objects connected to the lives of people in the past.

The vintage grandmother's clock chimed the hour, and Sophie realized with a start that it was time to open the shop. "I'll unlock the door."

"I can do it." Ruby stood.

"I got it." Sophie waved her friend back down, reaching the front door just as the clock stopped chiming.

With quick practiced moves, Sophie flipped the sign from Closed to Open and pulled up the shade, signaling that Timeless Treasures was open for business.

She turned back to Ruby. "Since my shift at the fairgrounds doesn't begin until noon, I thought I'd start going through the steamer trunk from the Wexman estate."

"You don't need to do that now," Ruby protested. "You're off duty, remember?"

"I've been looking forward to going through the trunk and the boxes since they were delivered." Sophie offered a happy sigh. "Every time I see an item from the past, I'm transported back to that time. I love getting these glimpses into other people's lives."

"It's kind of ironic, really."

Sophie gazed curiously at Ruby, not following. "What is?"

"The fact that überorganized, take-charge, get-everything-done Sophie gravitates to this kind of fantasy."

"I don't—"

"Just keep in mind that even better than catching glimpses into someone else's life is living your own." Ruby's expression turned serious. "You do too much for others and not enough for yourself."

Sophie was spared the need to respond when the phone in her pocket buzzed. She immediately snatched it up. Even though it had been two years since her father's stroke, any unexpected call sent her heart into overdrive. "This is Sophie."

"Soph, it's Dylan."

"Hey, you." She relaxed her death grip on the phone.

Though a call from Dylan was definitely unexpected, there was no cause for concern. Still, it was odd. In the two years they'd been dating, she could count on one hand the number of times he'd called her. Texting was his preferred method of communicating.

"About this volunteering gig..." Dylan paused. "Something has come up, and I won't be able to make it."

"Oh no." Concern filled Sophie's voice. She and Dylan had cleared their calendars so they could volunteer together at the fairgrounds. It had to be something serious for him to cancel at the last minute. "Is it your mom?"

For the past two weeks, Dylan's mother had been fighting a bad case of shingles.

"She's good. This has nothing to do with her."

"Are you—?"

He didn't give her a chance to finish.

"I'm fine. She's fine." He continued without pausing for breath. "Gage and Len are heading out to the lake today. Gage rented a boat for the weekend, and Len's parents are letting him use their cabin."

"But you—"

"Since I'm already off work until Monday, it seems meant to be." Dylan spoke quickly now. "You'll have fun listening to your history talks. I'll have fun at the lake. Win-win."

"We had plans." Sophie forced a light tone. "You agreed to volunteer."

"It's late notice. I get that. That's why I called instead of texting."

His breezy tone scraped against Sophie's nerves like a rusty blade.

Out of the corner of her eye, she saw Ruby cast her a curious glance.

"Dylan," Sophie mouthed back in answer.

With that one word, Ruby lost interest. Although Ruby was always pleasant to Dylan and never said anything against the man—okay, *rarely* said anything—it was clear her friend thought she could do better.

Lately, that same thought had begun to circle in Sophie's head. She refocused on her conversation with Dylan. "So, you called to let me know you aren't volunteering at all this weekend."

He hadn't mentioned the other days specifically, but Sophie could read between the lines.

"That's what I said." He sounded surprised. "Weren't you listening?"

"Just wanted to clarify." Sophie kept the irritation from her voice. At least she tried to. Didn't Dylan realize he wasn't just bailing on volunteering, he was bailing on her? "If you haven't already done it, I suggest you call Alcidean and let her know of your change in plans."

Dylan hesitated. "I thought you could do that."

Though Sophie liked Alcidean, the volunteer coordinator could be a hard-ass, which was likely the reason Dylan wanted Sophie to break the news to her.

"I'll give you her number." Sophie rattled it off. "Have fun this weekend."

She was on the verge of ending the call when he said her name in that deep, husky tone that had once turned her insides to mush.

"I realize this is a long shot, but I wish you'd consider coming with me. Gage's and Len's girlfriends will be there." His tone turned almost pleading. "You work all the time, Soph. Would it be so bad to do something just for fun? Just for us?"

For a second, Sophie was tempted. Dylan had a point. She'd put in a lot of hours at the store this past month, so they hadn't seen much of each other. That's why she'd been looking forward to spending this weekend with him.

"I'd love to, Dylan, I really would." Her voice held true regret. "But I promised to help at the fairgrounds."

When the call ended, Sophie leaned back against the counter.

"Let me guess." Ruby brought a perfectly manicured finger to her lips. "He's not coming."

Sophie waved an airy hand. "Something came up."

"You're not surprised he's not coming."

Sophie wanted to deny it, started to deny it, then shrugged instead. "I'll probably have more fun without him. Dylan isn't really into historical stuff."

Ruby's expression turned thoughtful. "When you're not

surprised that your boyfriend bails on you and you really don't care, that's an indication you're ready to be done dating."

"You know me, Ruby. I'm not the type of woman who needs to be attached at the hip with someone just because we're in a relationship." Sophie could have cheered when her voice came out casual and offhand, just as she'd intended.

"I'm not saying you have to be attached at the hip. I'm saying you should be able to count on your partner to show up for you." Ruby paused and appeared to choose her next words carefully. "Dylan knows how much you're looking forward to this weekend."

"We have different interests. I like history stuff. He likes sports. It's okay to have separate interests." Though she believed what she was saying, Sophie couldn't stop the wave of sadness.

"Okay, sure. I get that. But do you have any of the same interests? Wouldn't it be nice to have a partner you could actually share things with?"

Sophie thought of her parents, how they loved to cook together and had a shared passion for old movies.

"It would be nice," Sophie agreed, "but I'm not sure it's an absolute necessity. Besides, it's normal for romance in a relationship to fade as time goes on."

"It's been two years, not twenty. Besides, look at your parents. They're still thoughtful and romantic with each other."

"Yes," Sophie agreed. "Yes, they are." Ready to change the subject, she gestured toward the boxes at the end of the counter. "Enough talk about Dylan. I've got a few minutes before I need to leave for the fairgrounds. I can't wait a second longer to dig into the stuff from the Wexman estate and see what I bought."

"You were just at the auction last weekend." Ruby rose with an easy grace Sophie envied. "Surely you can't have already forgotten what you purchased."

"I'm honestly not sure what's in the boxes and trunk,"

Sophie admitted. "They came up at the end of a very long day when most of the serious bidders had left. No one remaining was particularly interested in bidding on them. I did it because I figured there's bound to be one or two things inside worth the price I paid. And this beauty..."

Leaning over, Sophie ran her hand along the rough and scarred, still-beautiful wood of the camelback top. "This steamer trunk was likely built between 1910 and 1920 and is a highly desirable piece. I sold a similar one last month for over $450. It wasn't in as good a shape as this one."

"You got a good deal."

"I got lucky." Sophie smiled. "You and I both know a good deal at an estate auction often depends on the size of the crowd and who is bidding."

She and Ruby started with the boxes. From the first box, they set aside a sunburst clock and a pair of gold-rimmed martini glasses. In the second, they discovered numerous pieces of costume jewelry that Sophie knew from past experience would sell quickly.

"Now, for the pièce de résistance." Crouching down, Sophie opened the trunk, surprised to find women's clothing from the early years of the twentieth century on top. She pulled out a spring dress covered in yellow flowers. "This is adorable. I love the way it narrows at the bottom, almost like a pencil skirt."

Ruby studied it. "With your dark hair, the dress is perfect for your coloring. It even looks like it might be your size."

Folding it carefully, Sophie set it and another dress in emerald green aside before lifting out a cream satin christening dress with scalloped lace trim.

Out of nowhere, an image of a baby with a swath of dark hair, bright blue eyes and a gummy smile flashed. An unexpected surge of longing had Sophie wanting to clasp the whisper-soft fabric tight against her chest. Instead, she refolded the gown and gently laid it atop the dresses.

A floral hatbox came next. But when Sophie opened the lid, she didn't find a hat. Instead, the box was filled with dozens and dozens of black-and-white family photographs from the early to mid-twentieth century.

Ruby picked up a few, shrugged, then dropped them back inside. "Kind of sad to think no one in the family wanted these."

Sophie felt a pang in the area of her heart. She found it incredibly difficult to toss away *any* photographs, even those of people she didn't know, but especially photos like these, which she saw as mini historical documents.

"I love to study the people in these images and imagine what was happening in their lives when the photograph was taken." Sophie reluctantly placed a photo back in the hatbox. "I'll go through these later when I have more time."

"Lookee, lookee, what have we here?" Ruby held up a small velvet drawstring pouch and gave it a shake. "Want to guess what's inside?"

Sophie cocked her head and considered. "A coin, maybe? Or a special piece of jewelry?"

"You only get one guess."

"I'll go with jewelry."

"I say coin." Ruby pushed the pouch into Sophie's hand. "Let's see which of us is right."

Loosening the drawstring, Sophie let the contents spill out onto the counter.

Ruby cackled—there was no other word for the sound she made—as she scooped up the gold coin.

"I win. Though something tells me this isn't worth enough to buy coffee at Starbucks." Her friend's brows drew together. "Whoa, what's this? The coin is normal on one side, but the other..."

Ruby flipped the coin back and forth, gazing at one side, then the other.

Sophie's heart skipped a beat when she saw the engraving. She nipped the coin from her friend's fingers. "Let me see."

Ruby leaned over her shoulder. "What do you think?"

"This isn't simply any coin." Sophie couldn't stop the smile that blossomed on her lips, or the heartfelt sigh that followed. "This is a love token."

"A what?" Ruby's eyes widened, then suspicion replaced the puzzlement. "Are you making that up?"

Sophie laughed and shook her head. "Love tokens were extremely popular up until the early twentieth century. Coins were sanded, usually only on one side, and then hand-engraved with words, images or initials. This love token has both words and some nicely carved intricate vines."

Interest sparked in Ruby's eyes. "What does it say?"

"'Love Be Yours, Love Be Mine,'" Sophie read, then showed Ruby the flowery script on the back of the coin. "That is so incredibly sweet."

"There's the romantic in you," Ruby teased.

Sophie lifted her chin. "What's wrong with wanting to find true love?"

"Nothing. Nothing at all. But if that's what you're looking for," Ruby slung an arm around Sophie's shoulders and gave a squeeze, "I'm telling you right now, you aren't going to find it with Dylan Connors."

2

GraceTown prided itself on providing a wide variety of experiences for its citizens. This year's four-day Chautauqua event had both locals and tourists flocking to the fairgrounds.

As traffic on the drive over had been relatively light, Sophie arrived twenty minutes early for her shift. Instead of rushing to check in and get her assignment, she gave herself permission to amble down the main walkway in the direction of the fairgrounds' administration building.

On the way, Sophie noticed two men on ladders stringing lights for the evening's festivities. Recognizing the younger one as a high school classmate, Sophie called out a greeting and offered a wave before continuing down the path.

The low-slung white frame building was in sight when Sophie paused to admire a patch of sunflowers in full bloom. According to a prominently displayed sign, the flowers had been planted—and were tended to—by a local 4-H chapter.

Just one more reason to love her community, she thought. In GraceTown, civic involvement began in childhood. Sophie had been in 4-H as a young girl, but hadn't thought of the organization in years. Perhaps there might be something she could do to help—

"Sophie."

Larry and Kathy Willis, close friends of her parents, were hurrying toward her. Sophie noticed that the couple had embraced the organizers' suggestion that attendees of the event wear period clothing.

Larry looked dapper in a slender-fitting brown suit and bow tie. A stylish fedora rested atop what he often laughingly referred to as his "chrome dome."

Kathy's cerulean blue dress and matching hat sporting a peacock feather flattered the woman's ivory complexion and brought out the blue in her eyes.

Sophie smiled. "Appears I'm not the only one ready to embrace all things Chautauqua."

"We're especially excited to hear Hazel Green speak." Kathy slanted a glance at her husband. "Aren't we, Larry?"

"Yes." Larry tugged at his collar. "I just didn't think it'd be so hot today."

"The good news," Sophie told Larry, "is there should be fans in the tents."

"That's excellent." Kathy, an attractive woman with a liberal amount of gray in her brown hair, inclined her head. "Your mother mentioned you were volunteering."

"I am." Happiness ran through Sophie like a pretty ribbon. "It should be a blast."

"I don't know how you do it all." Admiration shone in Larry's dark eyes. "You run a business, you volunteer, and I heard recently that you were appointed to the Economic Development Commission. Congratulations."

"Thank you. I'm pretty jazzed about it."

Though she'd indicated an interest in serving last year, the appointment two weeks ago had been a wonderful surprise.

"How are you going to find the time?" Kathy asked.

"I have a lot of energy." Sophie offered a good-natured shrug. "It's important for the small-business community to have a voice. I'm excited to be part of a group charged with identifying problem areas and making recommendations to the city council and mayor."

"You'll do a fine job." Larry gave a decisive nod. "They're lucky to have you."

"I'll certainly do my best." Sophie found herself warmed by the praise of a man who, even in his early seventies, still ran one of the largest—and most successful—construction companies in the area.

"—wouldn't know what to do without you," Kathy added.

Sophie was on the verge of admitting she'd missed part of what Kathy had said when Larry added, "Your parents are fortunate to have you in town. Our four are scattered across the country."

"I can't imagine living far away from them."

"You were a big help to your mom when Ned had his stroke." Kathy's expression sobered. "That was a scary time."

"It was." Sophie didn't want to revisit those memories. Even now, thinking of her father and how differently it could have turned out had her heart rate quickening.

Thankfully, they'd continued walking as they'd talked and now stood in front of the administration building. Sophie offered the couple a warm smile.

"I'm glad we ran into each other." She gestured to the building. "I'd love to chat more, but it's time for me to check in for my shift."

Kathy gave her a quick hug. "Tell your mom and dad we said hello."

"Will do." Once Sophie stepped inside the building, she stood for a moment, scanning the room.

The Formica-topped counter in front of her was chest-high. Half of the series of desks behind it were occupied.

Sophie quickly spotted Alcidean Lawless—GraceTown librarian and volunteer coordinator for this weekend's event—standing with a clipboard at the back of the room, talking to a woman Sophie didn't recognize.

She waited, letting the quiet buzz of conversation wash over her even as anticipation skittered up her spine. When she noticed Alcidean had concluded her conversation with the woman, Sophie stepped to the counter and lifted her hand to catch Alcidean's eye.

"Sophie." Weaving her way between desks like a running back on his way to the end zone, Alcidean gave Sophie a broad smile. "I'm so glad to see you."

"I'm excited about today."

"It should be fun for both of you." Alcidean glanced around, appearing to notice for the first time that Sophie had arrived alone. "Where's Dylan?"

That single question told Sophie he hadn't called.

"He's not coming." Sophie kept the disappointment from her voice. "I take it he didn't contact you?"

"He did not. I know you signed up to do this together." Confusion furrowed Alcidean's brow. "What happened? Is he ill? Was there a family emergency?"

Despite knowing this wasn't on her, Sophie felt the weight of Dylan's actions, or rather, lack of action. Though it might be easier to say he was sick, Sophie would not lie for him. Neither would she throw him under the bus.

"I'm not sure. I don't have the details." All true, Sophie assured herself. She didn't know Dylan's specific plans for each day or even which lake he was going to. "I'm disappointed, too."

Alcidean's gaze softened. "Don't worry. I'll deal with Dylan.

I'm just glad you're here, though I had no doubt that you'd show up. Everyone knows they can count on Sophie Jessup."

Sophie smiled graciously, accepting the compliment. "What will I be doing today?"

"Your assignment is one I think you'll like." For the first time, Alcidean appeared to notice Sophie's outfit. "Darling dress, by the way."

"Thank you." Sophie waited a couple of seconds, then prompted, "My assignment?"

"Oh, yes." Alcidean gave a little laugh. "My brain is going in a thousand different directions today. I assigned you to assist the event-planning staff by monitoring the presentations in the two tents."

"What's involved in monitoring?"

"Simply make sure the performances run smoothly and that the attendees and presenters are comfortable." Alcidean thought for a second. "This includes everything from providing the speakers with more water to adjusting the fans. Also, if anyone causes problems, you're to notify security immediately. Though I'm sure that won't happen."

"I'm sure not," Sophie agreed.

"The best part of your assignment is that it will allow you to watch the presentations."

"I appreciate that. Thank you." Alcidean's consideration only made Sophie feel worse about Dylan bailing at the last minute. She wondered what his job would have been. Perhaps she could do that job as well as hers. "Whatever Dylan's assignment was, I'd be happy to help—"

"I had him assisting you and picking up trash in the tents after each performance." Alcidean waved a dismissive hand. "If I can't find another volunteer to take over his duties, I'll call in one of the fairgrounds staff."

Sophie had no doubt those employees' plates were already filled to overflowing. She opened her mouth.

Alcidean must have sensed the protest coming, because she lifted a hand, and her gaze turned firm. "Don't worry about him, Sophie. Just do your job and enjoy the day."

WHILE SOPHIE WAS grateful that her straw hat kept the sun off her head, perspiration still slid down her back as she entered the first tent.

Someone had tied back the entrance flaps of the tent where the Hazel Green performance would be, obviously in hopes of facilitating air circulation.

After making small adjustments to where the two industrial-sized fans were pointed, Sophie stepped back into the heat and headed toward the second tent. She'd double-check that everything there was under control, then quickly grab something cold to drink before returning to the first tent to listen to Hazel Green.

Sophie stuck her hand into the pocket where she'd stashed a five-dollar bill, and her fingers brushed against something hard.

The love token.

Smiling, Sophie shoved both the money and the coin deeper into her pocket before turning toward the second tent and stepping inside. A preachers' quartet entertained the crowd with a rendition of "When the Roll Is Called Up Yonder."

From the research she'd done, she knew that historically a preachers' quartet would have been made up of only active clergy. Today's group included two retired ministers, a deacon and a local rabbi. Though the four men looked dapper in dark suits, crisp long-sleeved shirts and white bow ties, perspiration dotted their foreheads, and droplets of sweat slipped down their faces. Sophie's sympathy surged.

After making sure the water pitchers were full and that there were enough glasses for each performer, Sophie adjusted one of the fans, turning it so it pushed the air directly toward the quartet.

One of the ministers gave her a thumbs-up even as he continued to harmonize.

Smiling, Sophie headed outside. She came to an abrupt stop and frowned. Alcidean had specifically told her she would oversee two tents, not three. Strangely, Sophie could have sworn that third tent hadn't been there just minutes before, but that couldn't be. The ground crew couldn't possibly raise a tent so quickly. Sophie told herself that between the heat and her rush to get her tasks done, she must have simply missed it.

Even though she hadn't been assigned this third tent, if the performers inside needed her assistance, she would be here for them. The entrance flap was down, but when she lifted it and stepped inside, she found the interior decidedly cooler than the previous two.

She was struck by the fact that everyone inside, right down to the smallest child, was dressed in 1916 fashion.

The man speaking was portraying William Jennings Bryan, a popular orator on the Chautauqua circuit. Sophie had seen photos of Bryan. This guy could be his doppelgänger. The look and the mannerisms were classic Bryan.

From where she stood, the performer appeared comfortable and fully into his role. At the moment, he was giving Bryan's popular "Prince of Peace" lecture, and the audience appeared to be paying rapt attention.

In preparation for this weekend, Sophie had studied the Chautauqua movement, as well as those who would be speaking and performing this weekend. She hadn't stopped there. The town had chosen to feature the year 1916—before the United States entered WWI and before the 1918 Spanish flu pandemic —and Sophie had read all she could on that time period.

The 1910s had been a fascinating decade. There had been the founding of the Boy Scouts of America in 1910 and the horror of the Triangle Shirtwaist Factory fire in 1911. In 1916, Coca-Cola introduced its unique contour bottle.

She could sure use one of those Cokes right about now as she made her way through the crowd to check on conditions for the performer.

As she glanced around, Sophie wondered if this tent would remain up the entire four days of the Chautauqua, or if this was something special. If the speakers in this tent were here only to kick off the weekend, that might explain why Alcidean hadn't mentioned it.

Despite the tent's cooler interior, the large crowd was beginning to make Sophie feel slightly claustrophobic. She needed fresh air. Instead of leaving the way she'd come in, she spotted another exit just to her left. She moved as quickly and unobtrusively as she could in that direction and stepped out into the midday sun.

For a second, she swayed, as if she'd just stepped off a Tilt-A-Whirl. She waited until she felt steadier, then took a few steps forward and stopped, blinking. How had she missed this attraction of vintage cars, buggies and four-wheeled carriages? Especially considering how close it was to the tents.

The horse-drawn conveyances were interspersed with Model T's and other kinds of cars she couldn't identify.

She looked back. When she saw only one tent, not three, she felt the earth beneath her feet shift. Sophie tried to tell herself she must have gotten turned around when she'd come out of the last tent. That was the only logical answer.

She went back into the tent. While the performer used

expansive hand gestures to emphasize a point, she wove her way to the original entrance, her heart beating hard and fast.

But when she stepped outside, she wasn't back in modern-day GraceTown. Instead, she found herself still in an early-twentieth-century world where vendors manning booths offered everything from tintypes to ice cream.

Her head spun as she tried to make sense of the unexplainable. Sophie scanned the immediate area, searching for a place to sit where she could gather her thoughts. Her breath came out in a whoosh when she spotted an empty bench under the leafy branches of a large elm. Once she reached it, she collapsed onto the bench and took several calming breaths.

All around her were familiar signs of life that were, at the same time, unfamiliar. A Sousa march played in the distance, and the enticing scent of barbecued meat wafted on the air. Little girls wearing gingham dresses and wide hair ribbons giggled as they were handed ice cream cones advertised for eight cents.

What was happening? Had she passed out? Was this some kind of strange dream?

After a few moments and a couple of steadying breaths, Sophie took another look around. The sidewalk she'd strolled down less than an hour earlier was now a dirt path. The workers stringing lights when she'd arrived were nowhere in sight.

Nothing made sense.

"What is happening?" she cried in frustration. Her voice pitched high as panic spurted.

Several couples and a few individuals passing by cast curious glances in her direction, but didn't pause.

"Are you in distress, miss?"

Like a bucket of cold water, the inquiry had Sophie inhaling sharply and focusing on the person who'd said it.

A tall man with hair as dark as hers studied her, concern

etched across his handsome face. He was dressed, like everyone else she'd seen since exiting the tent, in clothing suitable for 1916.

In his white suit, striped blue Oxford shirt and red bowtie, he appeared cool, crisp and professional. Like her, he wore a straw hat.

Sophie was struck by the absurd thought that, with her blue dress, red tie and straw hat, they were a perfectly matched pair. Hysterical laughter bubbled up at the ridiculous thought, and some of the tension gripping her chest eased.

Or perhaps it wasn't the laughter easing her tension, but the man's reassuring smile and calm manner.

"Miss?" he prompted. "Is something wrong?"

"No, ah, no, I'm f-fine," she managed to stammer. "The heat—"

She didn't finish the comment. What could she say? *The heat is causing me to hallucinate? I'm seeing things that don't make sense?* Had she fallen and hit her head? Or passed out from the heat?

For whatever reason, she must be unconscious, and this was a dream. One in which a kind stranger took the time to make sure she was okay.

"It is exceedingly warm today," he agreed, his gaze watchful. "May I fetch your husband for you while you rest in the shade?"

"I-I'm not married," Sophie told him. "There is no one for you to fetch. Besides, I'm feeling steadier now."

He gave a nod.

Sophie sensed the man was only seconds away from strolling off and leaving her alone. Right now, he seemed like her one connection with reality. Even if that reality was a dream.

"My name is Sophia Jessup," she told him. "My friends call me Sophie."

"I'm Josiah Huston." He touched the brim of his hat. "It's a pleasure making your acquaintance, Miss Jessup."

"Please, call me Sophie."

He hesitated for a fraction of a second, then nodded. "You may call me Josiah."

Sophie cleared her throat. "Do you live in GraceTown, Josiah?"

"I do. I'm originally from Baltimore, but GraceTown is now my home."

"Do you have a wife and children?"

A shutter dropped over his eyes. "My wife passed away last year. We weren't blessed with children."

"I'm sorry to hear about your wife's death." Sophie gestured to a nearby bench in the shade. "Do you have time to sit with me for a spell?"

He opened his mouth as if to refuse the invitation, then said, "Thank you."

He waited for her to take a seat first, then he sat beside her.

"I haven't lost anyone close to me," she confided. "But I know the fear of it. My father had a serious health crisis two years ago. For a time, the doctors thought he might not live."

"I hope he's in good health now."

"He's doing well." Sophie smiled, then sobered. "I am sorry for your loss. Your wife must have been young."

"Twenty-two. I am—was—seven years older. Even now, it's still difficult to believe she's gone. Daisy was so vital and full of life."

"If you don't mind my asking, what happened?"

"Her appendix." Josiah spoke softly, almost to himself. "It ruptured. They operated, but the poison had spread throughout her body. The doctors insisted there was nothing they could do to thwart the infection."

"I'm so sorry." Sophie reached over and squeezed his hand.

She realized her mistake when a startled look crossed his face. She'd always found comfort in human contact. As she pulled back her hand, she reminded herself that not everyone—even strangers in a dream—felt that way.

"I suppose I should—" She paused. Should what? Go back into a tent that had brought her here, but wouldn't take her back?

Josiah's gaze turned sharp and assessing.

"You are suddenly very pale. May I get you something to drink? Perhaps an ice-cold Coca-Cola?" He lifted a hand before she had a chance to reply. "If you don't feel that sharing a soft drink with me would be proper, since we haven't been formally introduced, I understand."

The man had kind eyes. Of the other people who'd looked her way when she'd cried out, he was the only one who'd stopped to make sure she was okay.

Sophie decided that even in a dream, you had choices, and she chose to embrace the moment. "Something cold sounds absolutely wonderful."

When he rose to go, she stood.

"I'll be back," he assured her.

She smiled. "I'd like to come with you."

3

Josiah wasn't sure what to make of Sophia Jessup. She might be dressed like a proper young miss, but she possessed a bold spirit, one he found intriguing. He'd been shocked when she'd reached over to squeeze his hand with such familiarity.

But when he'd looked at her, there hadn't been flirtation in her eyes, only kindness.

How long had it been since he'd been touched by a woman, much less conversed with one for any length of time? Other than family, of course.

He stopped in front of an ice chest cooler. Slipping a hand into his pocket, he pulled put two coins, then turned to the young boy standing behind the cooler. "Two bottles of Coca-Cola, please."

Sophie smiled as she lifted the bottle from his fingers. "Thank you."

"Have you had a Coca-Cola before?" He paused. "The taste is unique, but pleasing."

"I have, and I like the taste very much." Sophie tipped the bottle to her red lips and took a long drink.

She didn't simply sip the liquid. She closed her eyes and let out a little sound of pleasure.

Something in Josiah stirred at the look of pure bliss on her face. He forced himself to look away as he drank from his own bottle.

"Thank you again."

He jerked when she touched his arm.

"I didn't realize just how much I needed that."

Her brilliant smile stole his breath, and he had to fight to find his words—an unfamiliar feeling for a man who prided himself on his elocution. "You're welcome."

Josiah took another long drink from the glass bottle and felt instantly refreshed. "Tell me about yourself, Miss Jessup."

"Sophie." She flashed a smile.

"As you wish." Josiah couldn't keep from smiling back.

"I work in a shop that sells antiques." She drank some more of the cola. "As I mentioned before, I'm not married, nor have I ever been. I enjoy the company of my friends and my parents. I love to read, especially about historical events."

Josiah also enjoyed such pursuits. Something told him if he took the time to get to know Sophie Jessup, he would discover they had even more in common than a love of history.

"What would your father think about you spending time with a man you just met, one with whom he is not acquainted?"

Sophie hesitated. "My parents trust me."

"Still, I can imagine they'd be concerned. If you'd like, I could..." He stopped, wondering what he'd been about to say. That they could stop over to her home so he could meet her parents? He wasn't courting her, didn't intend to court her. All he'd done was buy her a Coca-Cola.

"Like I said, they trust my judgment." She flashed a smile, her hazel eyes bright with interest. "What is it you do, Mr. Huston?"

"Josiah," he reminded her, then smiled. "My family sells motorcars, primarily for Ford. The Tin Lizzie touring car is our most popular model."

Sophie arched a brow. "Tin Lizzie?"

"Ford Model T."

"I noticed a lot of Tin Lizzies here." When she smiled up at him, he noticed with some relief that the color had returned to her cheeks. "Purchased no doubt from your dealership?"

"Highly likely. If not from the dealership here, then from the one my father runs in Baltimore," he admitted. "Though some may have been purchased directly from the factory. At one point, we were having difficulty getting enough vehicles to meet demand. But when Mr. Ford had his factory move to an integrated moving assembly line, which allowed workers to build a car in one and a half hours instead of twelve and a half, the shortage eased." Josiah clamped his mouth shut when he realized he'd been rambling.

"That's a huge difference." Sophie handed her empty bottle to the boy by the ice chest, and Josiah did as well.

When she took his arm, he felt the warmth of her touch all the way through his jacket. She smelled good, too, like oranges. "Do you recall how you felt the first time you rode in a motorized vehicle?"

Josiah pulled his brows together, not understanding. "How I felt?"

"Yes. Were you scared? Excited? Or perhaps a little sad that horses and buggies were on their way out?"

The rapid-fire questions, or maybe it was her bright-eyed gaze filled with interest, made him smile.

"I was excited." Josiah paused and considered, intent on being completely honest. "Perhaps a bit apprehensive initially, because of the speed. I was ten. My father reassured me the motor wagon was safe and eased my fears by explaining how the vehicle worked."

A soft look filled Sophie's eyes. "Sounds as if you and your dad enjoy a close relationship."

Josiah nodded. Though they often disagreed on business matters, he had great respect for his father. "My father is an honorable man."

"Tell me your best memory of him." Sophie offered him an encouraging smile.

"For what purpose?"

She shrugged. "I'm curious."

Josiah rubbed his chin. The time that had come to mind wasn't one he wanted to revisit. In fact, he hadn't spoken of that day to anyone.

"The night that," he swallowed past the lump that rose in his throat, "Daisy passed away, my father sat with me at her bedside in the hospital while I waited for the undertaker to arrive."

Surprise flickered in her eyes, followed quickly by compassion. "Did he comfort you?"

"If you're asking if he consoled me with words during that time, the answer is no." How could he explain that simply having his father with him had been a comfort? "It was enough for him to be there."

Her expression turned somber. "I imagine so."

"What about you?" Josiah was determined to shift the conversation to her. After all, he knew all there was to know about himself. "What is your best memory of your father?"

Sophie brought a finger to her lips, drawing his attention to her red mouth as she pondered the question.

"The first time he took me fly-fishing." Those luscious lips curved. "My mother thought I was too young at the time, but he knew I could handle it."

Josiah knew what fly-fishing entailed. He couldn't imagine

his sisters wanting to be involved in such a sport, or for that matter, his father encouraging such an interest.

Now his mother...

“Oh my goodness, look at them.” Sophie pointed. Her smile widened.

Josiah turned to see four couples roller-skating down the concrete walkway, sending those strolling scurrying out of the way. The men and women laughed and talked with reckless abandon.

“That looks like fun.” Her tone held a wistful quality.

“Do you know how to roller-skate?” Despite the wistfulness he’d heard, Josiah wasn’t sure why he’d asked. He had no doubt that while he sat alone in his big, empty house, Sophie would be out skating and pursuing other equally adventurous activities.

“I used to roller-skate when I was a little girl.” Her expression turned pensive.

"Now?"

Her dark brows pulled together. “Now I suppose there isn’t much I do purely for fun.” A small sigh escaped her lips. “I’ve been told I put in too many hours at work.”

“I have been told the same thing by my family.”

“Is it true?” Sophie asked.

“Since Daisy’s passing, I prefer being at the dealership. The house is empty without her.”

Sympathy shimmered in her eyes. “I can understand that.”

“Why are you always working?” The instant Josiah asked, he wished he could pull the question back. He was aware it wasn’t easy for an unmarried woman to make a living, with most working as servants or factory workers.

As if she’d read his mind, Sophie shook her head. Her hair, the color of rich walnut, caught the light. “I don’t work all the hours that I do because I *have* to, but because I *want* to. I love what I do. I’ve tried explaining that to my parents and friends, but—" She lifted her hands, then let them drop. "They still badger me to take more time for myself."

"They should be happy, then."

She offered a tentative smile. "I don't understand."

"That's what you're doing today." He gestured widely with one hand to indicate the happy scene laid out before them. "You're enjoying a Coca-Cola and taking time for yourself."

A slow smile spread across her face. "You're absolutely right."

They walked for several feet in silence. Then she stopped and cocked her head. "Such a sweet sound."

For a second, Josiah was confused, and then he realized she was listening to a mockingbird singing in a nearby tree.

When she noticed him staring, her cheeks turned bright pink. "Like I said, I'm usually much too busy to appreciate simple pleasures."

As they resumed walking, he watched Sophie study the vendor stands as if she'd never seen them before.

Then he realized it wasn't the stands or the merchandise that captivated her, but the people—the man in the white apron dispensing ice cream, the photographer with the handlebar mustache taking photographs, the variety of patrons shopping at each of the stands.

Her keen interest made no sense, considering she must have traveled through this area earlier on her way to the exhibition tent. "What speakers have you heard today?"

"Mr. Bryan. He was giving his 'Prince of Peace' speech," she told him. "It was very crowded inside the tent, so I stepped out."

"My father took me with him to hear Mr. Bryan give his 'Cross of Gold' speech. He is an electrifying orator."

"He had the crowd electrified today." Inclining her head, Sophie gazed up at him. "Did you come here today hoping to hear a particular speaker?"

"A couple of them."

He could see he'd piqued her interest, and that made him smile.

"Who?" she pressed.

"Lucy Branham, for one."

Surprise skittered across Sophie's face. "She was raised in Baltimore. Have you heard her before?"

"Last year. She and her mother both spoke at a rally held in Baltimore."

"She picketed the White House."

"I don't recall hearing that, but she is a dynamic orator." Josiah thought back to last year's rally. His father had refused to go, so Josiah had attended with his mother.

If he hadn't, Josiah had no doubt Clara Huston would have gone alone, the way she had several years earlier when over a thousand suffragists organized a parade and marched west on Monument Street. "I feel certain Miss Branham's speech this year will be much the same as when I heard her last. She spoke of the decades-long fight to win the right to vote for women. A fight that continues."

"Were you the only man in the audience?"

"No. There were husbands there, but by far the majority of those in attendance were women. My mother ardently believes that women, like men, deserve all the rights and responsibilities of citizenship." He studied her for a long moment. "Some women, and many men, do not agree with that viewpoint. They feel women should concentrate on their role in the domestic sphere."

"Change—even change for the better—can be scary to some," Sophie admitted. "This change will happen."

Her fervent tone brought the smile back to his lips. "I take it you believe as my mother does?"

"I do."

A warmth traveled through him at the fire in her eyes. Many women called Clara Huston a suffragist, as if that was a bad thing. He was proud of his mother for standing up for her beliefs. Slanting a sideways glance at the woman at his side, he had a feeling she and his mother would get along splendidly.

"What about your wife? Was Daisy also a suffragist?"

Josiah shook his head.

"What else can you tell me about Josiah Huston?"

"I'm not being modest when I say there is not all that much to tell." As Josiah viewed it, he'd traveled a simple road, up to this point. "I grew up in Baltimore, attended St. John's College in Annapolis, then returned home after graduation. As I mentioned, my father has an automobile dealership there. I became his right-hand man. He is a fair man, but a bit old-fashioned in his approach to business."

Sophie's hazel eyes brightened. "How so?"

Josiah hesitated, not wanting to speak ill of any man, especially when that man was his father. "He is an astute businessman, but he can be tight-fisted with his money. Especially in regards to those he employs."

"You don't agree with some of his business practices."

That was an understatement. The way his father dealt with his employees had been one of the reasons Josiah had happily moved to GraceTown to take control of his own dealership.

"He pinches every penny, which he believes is the reason the Baltimore dealership is so profitable." Josiah chose his next words carefully, not wanting Sophie to get the wrong impression. "My father is a wonderful man, a loving husband and father who has worked hard and achieved much success."

"But?" Sophie prompted.

"I concur with Mr. Ford in that I believe in paying those who work for me a living wage."

"Are you referring to Mr. Ford's 'five-dollar day' plan?"

"Yes." Josiah told himself he shouldn't be surprised she was aware of the plan. In the short time they'd conversed, he'd learned that not only was Sophie exceedingly pleasing to the eye, with her shiny dark hair and hazel eyes, but she also had an inquisitive and sharp mind.

"If I'm remembering correctly," Sophie's brows furrowed in thought, "in order to earn the full amount, the workers have to maintain certain standards of efficiency, and they need to stay on the job for, what, a year?"

"Six months." Josiah nodded. "I'm implementing a version of those standards with my staff here in GraceTown."

"Isn't paying top dollar a risk when your business is new to this community?"

He heard no judgment in her tone, only curiosity. "I believe in my employees. I want them to succeed. If they do an excellent job, I succeed."

"I like you, Josiah Huston." Lips that reminded him of ripe strawberries curved. "I really like how you think."

Startled by the proclamation, Josiah wasn't sure how to respond. Such familiarity wasn't common when two people had just become acquainted. While he was still contemplating his response, she studied him intently.

"You might be shocked to know that I've never ridden in a Model T."

She might have phrased that as a statement, but her eyes held a question.

"I have mine here at the fairgrounds." Josiah spoke cautiously, not wanting to overstep. "I would be honored to take you for your first spin in one."

The bright smile she flashed arrowed straight to his heart.

For the first time since Daisy had passed, Josiah felt the stirring of interest in a woman. It wasn't simply that Sophie was beautiful—Josiah was acquainted with many lovely women—

but Sophie was also different. Her spirit, her joie de vivre, came through so strongly it enveloped him in its glow.

"I realize you came to listen to the speakers," she said. "I don't want to take you away from them."

"I would much rather take a spin in my Tin Lizzie." He placed a hand on her arm and met her eyes. "With you."

4

As Sophie strode with Josiah toward the tent, she didn't take his arm again.

She thought about it. She seriously considered it. This was, after all, her dream—or maybe her hallucination—so why deprive herself? But she kept her hands to herself. For now.

A performance must be about to start, because streams of people were filing into the tent. Sophie wondered if Lucy Branham, the woman Josiah had specifically wanted to see, was the next speaker.

He didn't even glance in the direction of the tent.

"Is Lucy Branham speaking now?"

Josiah paused and pulled out what Sophie recognized as an 18K gold Elgin pocket watch. A floral motif and a pie crust edge decorated the front cover, which sprang open to reveal the white porcelain dial. "Yes. She should be onstage within ten minutes."

"Do you want to—?"

"I'd rather take you for a ride." Josiah hesitated. "Unless you'd prefer to stay and listen?"

"I'd rather go for a ride."

"Then that's what we'll do." Josiah strode over and stopped

beside a shiny black car. Until now, Sophie had seen such cars only in museums. He rested a hand on the black fender. "This is a 1916 Ford Model T."

"It's gorgeous." Though the Tin Lizzie was different than the cars Sophie knew and drove, there was a beauty in its simplicity. If she remembered correctly, it was that simplicity that had made it easy to be mass-produced. "Were there many changes from the 1915 model?"

"There are several." Josiah's tone turned businesslike, as if she were a potential customer. "The headlight and cowl lamp rims went from brass to painted black steel. I believe Mr. Ford made the change because the price of brass has been soaring due to the war in Europe."

"World War I," Sophie murmured.

Knowing that both a world war and a pandemic were coming had her heart twisting—until she remembered this was a dream.

"Pardon?"

"The war in Europe impacts the entire world."

"It does indeed." Josiah hesitated.

Sophie saw he wanted to say more, but battles and casualties probably weren't topics a man of his time discussed with a woman, much less one he'd only recently met.

Josiah gestured to the car. "The transmission cover is now cast iron instead of aluminum, and there are smooth-surfaced pedals. The fuel tank is under the front seat."

As Josiah pointed out other changes, Sophie strolled around the car. Simply listening to his deep voice made her happy. His enthusiasm for the car and its "modern" features was contagious.

Sophie bet Josiah was not only a stellar boss, but an extraordinary salesman.

"There are two ways to start the vehicle," he told her when

he stopped in front of the Model T. "Cranking—that's the crank right in front of you—or by the electric start."

"Can I see what cranking looks like?" Sophie couldn't hide her excitement. This was the best dream she'd ever had, and she wasn't in any hurry to have it end.

"You're really interested." He sounded surprised.

"I really am."

Josiah's smile flashed.

Her heart skipped a beat.

"It would be my pleasure."

Josiah strode over to the driver's side of the car and reached inside. "First, I make sure the key is off and the handbrake locked."

Once that was done, he joined her at the front of the car. "I'm going to use my left hand with my thumb underneath. That way, in case of backfire it will push my hand off, but not break my arm."

After glancing over to make sure he had her attention, he leaned down to grab the crank.

He had her full attention all right. Since his focus was on the car, Sophie let her gaze travel up his lean, muscular body. Though his trousers were looser than modern fashion dictated, she could tell he had a really nice backside.

She briefly let her gaze drop to his leather shoes before slowly traveling it upward again, until she reached the straw hat atop his dark hair.

At the lake, Dylan was likely wearing board shorts and a short-sleeved shirt that showed off his muscular arms and legs. Though she had to admit shorts would be cooler today, Sophie found she liked Josiah's more formal appearance and leaner build.

A swift crank had the car sputtering to life.

Josiah looked up and grinned.

When their eyes met, everything in Sophie melted.

His eyes were clear and so very blue. There was no guile there, at least none that she could see. Sophie already knew this wasn't a man who would blow off a commitment to go play with his friends, no matter how tempting the offer.

This was a man she could trust, which was why she didn't have any hesitation about getting into the car with him, even though they'd just met. Especially since this was only a dream.

If she got frightened, Sophie figured she would simply force herself to wake up—like she'd done last week when she'd dreamed she was being attacked by a dog.

She'd needed that dream to be over.

This dream, on the other hand... Well, this was definitely one to savor.

Josiah rounded the front of the car to the passenger side, opened the door and held out a hand. She stared, not sure what he wanted. Then she realized he was offering to assist her into the car.

The assistance proved helpful because of the unwieldiness of her dress. His clean-shaven face drew close as he helped her get settled in the passenger seat, and she caught the enticing scent of sandalwood.

Sophie tried to recall details about cologne or aftershave in this time period and came up empty. Regardless of the origin of the scent, Josiah smelled terrific. "You smell good."

"Thank you." A startled look crossed his face. Then his gaze met hers. "As do you."

Satisfaction surged, and Sophie automatically reached for the seat belt before realizing there wasn't one. It appeared historical details were important enough to her to be accurate even when she was dreaming. She gave a little laugh.

Josiah, who'd closed her door and gotten behind the wheel, glanced at her, a questioning look in his eyes.

"It's crazy. This morning, I never imagined I'd get to ride in a Tin Lizzie today." She flung her arms wide. "Yet, here I am."

Josiah's lips curved. "When I arose this morning, I never imagined I'd be taking a beautiful woman for a drive."

He really did have a lovely smile, Sophie thought.

"Then I say, this is a lucky day, and we should make the most of it," Sophie declared.

He did some things with the controls, and the car moved forward over the uneven grass before he turned it onto a dirt roadway.

"I'm curious what 'make the most of it' entails." Josiah slanted a quick glance at her before refocusing on the road.

"Enjoy every moment." Sophie stretched her right hand out of the windowless car, catching the breeze. The air felt incredibly good against her face. Though her hat was straw and had done an admirable job of keeping the sun from her face, she didn't need to continue to wear it while in the car.

With one sweeping gesture, it was off her head and on her lap. After raking her fingers through her hair, she shook her head and had the loose curls tumbling haphazardly around her shoulders.

Surprise skittered across Josiah's face. "What are you doing?"

"I'm making the most of the day." She grinned and tipped her head back, reveling in the breeze. "This feels so much better."

"I've never known anyone quite like you, Miss Jessup."

Sophie laughed and shot him a teasing smile. "Do I need to put my hat back on for you to call me Sophie?"

Josiah laughed, the sound rusty, as if he hadn't laughed in a long time. "Sophia."

"Now I know you're teasing me."

"Don't you like your given name?"

"I like it very much," she told him quite honestly. "It's just that I've always gone by Sophie."

"Your given name is beautiful. It means wisdom."

The fact that he would know such a trivial detail surprised her. "How do you know that?"

"I have a great-aunt named Sophia. I don't know her well."

"If her name is Sophia, I'm sure she's a lovely person."

He said nothing, but the look on his face had her laughing. "I take it she's not a lovely person."

"She's my father's aunt." He made the pronouncement as if that settled the matter.

"Just because she's related doesn't mean she's nice." Sophie offered Josiah an impish grin. "Tell me what she's like." She lifted her hands. "I promise not to take offense even though we share the same name."

Josiah hesitated. "According to those who know her best, she's sharp-tongued and critical. Thankfully, she lives far away. Despite all that, my mother considered naming my youngest sister Sophia because she liked the name. She chose Edith instead."

"That makes sense to me." Sophie nodded. "To my way of thinking, if you use the name of someone you know for your child, it should be someone who evokes pleasant memories."

"I agree." Josiah's chuckle took her by surprise. "Who knows? You may end up changing my feelings about Sophia."

She liked the way her name rolled off his tongue. Or maybe it was the warmth behind it. Or the look in his eyes when he spoke it.

"I hope so," she told him.

"Now that we have that out of the way." Josiah glanced at the hat on her lap. "Tell me what else we can do to make the most of the day."

5

When Josiah had risen that morning, his day had been precisely planned out. The day had begun with calisthenics and strength training. The area he'd set up in his home contained everything from skipping ropes and medicine balls to an assortment of barbells and dumbbells.

After vigorous exercise and a visit to his newly installed needle-nose shower, Josiah had dressed for the day and headed to the kitchen. Though he had a housekeeper/cook who prepared his evening meals, he preferred his morning solitude.

Before he and Daisy had moved in, he'd had the kitchen updated with all modern appliances. The Boss glass door-oven and Kelvinator electric refrigerator had made her clap her hands and give him a big kiss. The funny thing was, the item he and Daisy had both ended up loving most was the electric percolator.

While he'd enjoyed a breakfast of shredded wheat biscuits and cream and drunk his coffee, Josiah had read the newspaper. It was a habit he'd developed very young. When his father would set down a section of *The Baltimore Sun*, Josiah would pick it up.

Both of his parents prided themselves on being knowledgeable about current events. Josiah had to admit that lately he'd experienced increasing concern over what was going on in Europe.

He had the feeling that President Wilson would soon bring the country into the fray. He'd planned to stop by the fairgrounds to listen to Mr. Bryan's speech before Miss Branham took the podium, but several potential customers had prevented him from making it to the first lecture.

By the time Josiah had concluded his conversation with the men, Mr. Bryan's speech had been well under way. He'd been hurrying to the tent when he'd noticed Sophie.

Something about her had drawn his eye. That some intangible something had had him pausing his long strides and changing direction. She'd appeared lost and alone. Josiah knew that feeling. It was how he felt every day since Daisy's passing.

It might not have been proper for a single man to approach a woman alone, but he hadn't been able to simply walk past her if she'd needed help.

Now, sitting in a rowboat in the middle of Culler Lake, with the sun shining brightly in the blue sky, Josiah felt fully alive for the first time in over a year.

As he watched, Sophie closed her eyes and tipped back her head. With dark curls tumbling around her shoulders, long lashes fanning her cheeks and full lips curved into a smile, she stole his breath.

Josiah studied Sophie's generous mouth and the soft curves the simple sailor dress couldn't fully hide and fought a surge of desire.

What was he doing here with her?

He wasn't courting her, Josiah reassured himself. Enjoying the company of a beautiful woman for an afternoon wasn't courting. Though he had to admit Sophie was more than a pretty face. She was intelligent, kind and a pleasure to be around. Josiah recalled her animation when she'd told him that making the most of the day meant doing things that were fun, things you might not do at another time.

"Josiah."

He blinked, realizing that while his mind had been wandering, she'd opened her eyes.

"You were right," he blurted.

She smiled. "I usually am. What was I right about this time?"

Taking a hand off the oar, he gestured widely. "About the importance of doing something enjoyable. Inside, I feel as calm as these waters."

"I feel much more relaxed as well."

They exchanged a smile.

"The ride in the car was amazing." Sophie glanced around as if taking it all in. "So much open countryside. I'd forgotten how small GraceTown was back..."

She stopped herself, then let her gaze drift over the smooth surface of the water. "I've never been in a rowboat before."

She'd said that when they'd been driving past the lake. He'd impulsively pulled over the car. When he'd first moved to GraceTown, a customer had informed him that the rowboat perched at the water's edge was there for anyone to use.

He'd planned to take Daisy out here, but he'd been busy setting up the new business, and time had gotten away from him. Then it had been too late.

"This day is exactly what I needed." Sophie met his gaze. "Thank you."

"I should be thanking you."

She cocked her head, confusion in her pretty hazel eyes. "What did I do?"

"I'm not the most spontaneous man." His lips lifted in a smile. "I have been today, and I like how that feels."

"I'm glad. I'm loving every minute of our adventure." She flung her arms out and breathed in deeply, the action pulling the bodice of her dress tight against her breasts.

As feelings long buried stirred, Josiah forced his gaze away with great effort.

"I'm starting to realize that I don't take enough time to simply be in the moment," she went on. "Life can be so hectic. It's easy to get caught up in my work and forget to enjoy other things in life, like a beautiful day and the company of a new friend."

Her words were a solid blow to his heart. He knew all too well what it was like to get caught up in the day-to-day, especially when launching a business. He also knew the resultant high price.

Josiah blew out a long breath, and before he realized what he was doing, he gave voice to his regrets.

"Those months after Daisy and I moved to GraceTown were busy ones. We had purchased a home here and done some remodeling. Daisy was busy decorating. I was driving back and forth to Baltimore regularly. My mind was consumed by all that needed to be done. She'd mentioned feeling poorly off and on, but blamed the intermittent nausea and pain in her belly on something she'd eaten. As she had a delicate constitution, I didn't think much of it." Josiah shifted his gaze away from Sophie's searching gaze. "If I'd paid closer attention and gotten her to the doctor sooner, her appendix wouldn't have ruptured, and the infection—"

Sophie's hand closing over his took him by surprise and stilled his words. When he attempted to pull back, she tightened her grip. "You can't go there, Josiah. Second-guessing your actions is a dead-end road that will bring nothing but regret and heartache."

"You don't understand." He told himself to try again to pull his hand back, that it wasn't proper, but the simple human touch reached inside and soothed the raw space in his heart.

"I do understand."

He shook his head. "You can't—"

"Before my father had his stroke, he mentioned several times that he had a headache and felt light-headed." Sophie's eyes grew dark with memories. "I was busy, and I didn't pay much attention. I should have made him go to the doctor."

"What about your mother?" Josiah asked.

Sophie blinked. "What about her?"

"I assume they live in the same house." Josiah knew nothing went on in his parents' home that his mother didn't know about.

"Yes."

"Does she also ask herself those same questions that lay so heavy on your heart?" He gentled his tone, sensing there was no need to push. Sophie was an intelligent woman who could make the connection.

Her gaze grew thoughtful, and he could tell she was looking back. "She urged him to see a doctor, but he insisted the light-headedness was due to not eating regularly."

He met her gaze. "If your mother, the woman he lived with, who undoubtedly saw him more and knew him better than anyone, couldn't get him to see a physician, how could you have?"

Sophie didn't speak for a long moment. Then she let out a long breath and nodded. "I see where you're going with this, and you're right."

Picking up the oars, Josiah began rowing. He was happy he'd been able to help relieve her mind. He knew the heavy weight of guilt and how carrying it around could wear you down.

"What about Daisy?" she asked abruptly.

He stopped rowing. "What about her?"

"It sounds as if your family is a close one."

Still wary, he studied her. "We are."

"Did her family also live in Baltimore?"

Josiah nodded. "Her parents live there, as well as her three sisters."

"None of them noticed her feeling poorly?"

It was a simple question, one for which he should have had a ready answer. But he didn't.

"I hope you do not think that I'm suggesting you shift blame," Sophie added quickly when he didn't respond.

"Then why bring up her family and mine?"

Her hazel eyes were clear and direct when they rested on his face. "I believe it helps to remember we are not alone in our regret."

Josiah wished he could derive comfort from her words, but he found none.

"I appreciate you wanting to help." The acknowledgment sounded stiff and formal, even to his own ears.

If she noticed, Sophie gave no indication. "Tell me about her."

He gave his head a little shake.

"My mother..." Sophie paused and appeared to choose her words carefully. "One of the things she does is to help people who have lost someone they loved. She believes that talking about that person can help the one left behind find a sense of peace. I'm not asking because I'm nosy, but because I'm genuinely interested in knowing what Daisy was like. I know she had to be someone special for you to have loved and married her."

"Your mother is a social worker."

"A type of social worker, yes." Sophie offered an encouraging smile.

Would it help him to speak of Daisy? Daisy's parents found it too painful to speak of her. Even his own parents shifted the conversation whenever he brought her up. It was starting to feel as if she'd never existed at all. "What do you want to know?"

"How did you meet? What was she like? What did she like to do?"

"My sister introduced us." Josiah's lips curved at the sweet memory. "She and Edith met at a church social and quickly became bosom friends."

"What was Daisy like?"

In Josiah's limited experience, women didn't want to discuss another woman with a man, unless that other woman was a relative. Still, Sophie had asked and appeared genuinely interested. "Daisy was quiet. She preferred to listen rather than speak. But she was intelligent and had the best sense of humor." He chuckled, remembering an incident that had happened the day he'd first met Daisy.

Sophie leaned forward. "Tell me what happy memory brings that smile to your lips."

"Not long after meeting her, Edith invited Daisy to the house for dinner one Saturday night. During the course of the conversation, Edith mentioned a musical soiree my parents were hosting the same night." Josiah would never forget that first glimpse of Daisy. "Daisy thought Edith had invited her to the soiree, so she came dressed to the nines, while everyone else was dressed for a quiet family meal. I thought she was the most beautiful woman I'd ever seen."

Sophie grimaced. "Was Daisy embarrassed?"

"If she was, she didn't let on." He shook his head, the memory warm and sweet. "That's when I decided I wanted to get to know her better. She impressed everyone with her composure."

Josiah paused and let the memories of that evening wrap around him like a favorite sweater. "Every single person in my family adored her."

"That's important. Especially if you're close to your family."

A look he couldn't quite decipher crossed Sophie's face.

"I've been seeing a man my parents don't particularly like," she said. "It's made things awkward."

"Why don't they like him?"

Sophie's dark brows drew together in thought. "They don't think he treats me well."

Anger surged through Josiah's veins, surprising him with the intensity. Yet, when he spoke, his voice was as smooth as the surface of the lake. "In what way?"

"He often cancels at the last minute, even when we made the plans weeks before." Sophie chewed on her bottom lip. "I don't want to say it's usually if something better comes up, but it feels that way."

"Something better?" Josiah forced a casual tone. "Perhaps giving me an example would help me understand the situation more clearly."

Indecision warred on her face before she finally nodded. "Here is an example. Last month, we were supposed to attend the birthday party of one of my closest friends. He'd known about the party for weeks, and I was looking forward to introducing him to some of the people who would be there that he hadn't yet met."

"He agreed to escort you."

"Yes." Sophie gave a decisive nod. "It was on his calendar."

Josiah puzzled at the odd choice of words, but he understood the sentiment. He relaxed back in the boat and waited for her to continue. There was no reason to rush.

"Then he got tickets to watch the Orioles play—great seats. And he hadn't been to a ball game yet this year. He was very excited." Sophie glanced away.

The picture was becoming clear. "I'm deducing that the game was played at the same time as the party."

"Your deduction is correct." Sophie shrugged. "He did ask me if I'd like to go to the game with him. I couldn't, not and skip Ruby's party. She's my closest friend, and even if she wasn't—"

"You'd promised her you'd be there." He met her gaze. "You are a woman of your word."

"I am." She lifted her hands. "We both know there are times when circumstances beyond our control keep us from doing something we promised we'd do. Barring the unforeseen, I keep my word."

"A person's word should be their bond." Josiah gave an approving nod. "You attended your friend's party."

"I did. I had a really fabulous time." Her smile was back. "There were several friends I hadn't seen in years. The only downside was that Dylan wasn't with me, and I had to explain why he wasn't."

"What did you tell everyone?"

"The truth." She glanced down at her hands before her gaze returned to him. "I wasn't about to lie. I simply said that he'd gotten tickets to watch the O's play and was excited about going."

"I'm sure they understood." Josiah made the effort to be gallant.

"Actually, they didn't." She laughed. "Oh, some of the men appeared to, of course, but Ruby didn't have much use for him before, and that action clinched her feelings."

"She was angry because he didn't come to her party?"

Sophie gave a snort. "She didn't care about that. She knew I'd wanted him there and was upset that he'd ditch me like that."

"Ditch?"

"That he would change plans at the last minute."

Josiah nodded his understanding. "The same reason your parents weren't fond of him. Because he'd 'ditch' you."

Josiah wasn't certain if it was his use of the unfamiliar word that made her smile, he only knew he liked seeing the smile back on her lips.

"Yes," she said. "It's becoming clearer that he isn't the man for me."

Something about the way she made the pronouncement, or maybe it was the words she used, had him wondering if this man was still her beau.

"Is he still courting you?" Josiah wasn't about to spend time with a woman, no matter how innocent that time, who was being actively courted and accepting the attentions of another.

"Dylan has been in my life for some time, but I don't think I love him." Sophie hesitated. "Then again, I'm not sure I know what love feels like."

"I knew I loved Daisy the moment I saw her." Josiah spoke solemnly as if repeating a vow. "That love only grew and deepened the more that we were together."

"You never once doubted that it was love you felt for her?"

"No." He laid a hand on her arm. "When it's right, you will know. You won't have any doubts."

Sophie's hazel eyes, glowing gold in the sunlight, never left his face. Then, without warning, she leaned forward and pressed her lips to his.

Josiah's lips, warm from the sun, were firm and smooth, and Sophie instantly knew one kiss wasn't going to be enough.

Her arms stole around his neck as the kiss took on a life of its own. She'd just opened her mouth to his, anticipating the smooth slide of his tongue against hers, when he pulled back.

A second later, he was disentangling her arms from his neck.

Cheeks burning, Sophie sat back. For a moment, she chastised herself. This wasn't modern-day GraceTown, but an era in which proper young ladies were more circumspect about their desires.

Still, she'd never in her entire twenty-nine years been so completely charmed by a man. Besides, this was her dream. Shouldn't she be able to kiss anyone she wanted?

From the look of startled surprise on Josiah's face, apparently not. Which meant an apology was due. Sophie sighed. "I'm sorry. I didn't mean to jump you."

"Jump me?"

"Kiss you like that." She gave a rueful laugh. "I mean, I did want to kiss you, but I know that isn't the way for a proper young lady to behave."

"I enjoyed kissing you. But," he gestured with his head, "we are also not alone."

Sophie spotted the canoe in the distance. Thankfully, both parties in the boat appeared more focused on reaching the shore than trying to see what was happening in a random rowboat.

"I won't—"

His knuckles, gently sliding down the side of her cheek, stopped the promise that she hadn't wanted to make in midsentence.

"I hope it happens again, Sophia Jessup." He smiled. "I like kissing you. I enjoy being with you."

"I like being with you, too." Relief slid through her as she returned his smile. "Simply being with you today is the best dream I've ever had. I've never felt like this about anyone before."

Normally, if she'd just met a guy, such a declaration would never have happened. If she had been so foolish to give away her feelings on the first date, the pronouncement would have had him running for the hills.

But this was a dream, and Josiah was her dream man. Crazy as it sounded, right here, right now, it felt as if he was the man she'd been searching for her entire life. The connection between them was so powerful that she wanted nothing more than to wrap her arms around him and never let go.

"I had planned on working today." Even as he spoke the words, he began rowing toward shore. "After the presentations."

Sophie's heart sank. It appeared that even in her dreams, speaking from the heart wasn't the way to go.

"However, I am having such an enjoyable time that I can't bear to see it end." He hesitated. "I don't know if you have other obligations this afternoon, but if you do not, I would like very much if you would consider spending the rest of the day with me."

Sophie's heart gave an excited leap. If she were awake, she'd be busy with the fair and the shop and her family and a seemingly endless to-do list. In this dream, none of that existed. She was free to enjoy Josiah for as long as the dream lasted. "I have no obligations, and I would very much enjoy spending more time with you. What is it you have in mind?"

The boat reached the shore, and he stepped out, then extended a hand to her. "There's an area not far from here bursting with wildflowers. I thought perhaps we could start with a walk."

Simple pleasures, Sophie thought. How many times had her mother urged her to embrace the simple pleasures in life?

Well, today she would do just that.

Sophie placed her hand in Josiah's. "I can't think of anything I'd like more than walking through a field of wildflowers with you."

6

Sophie realized that Josiah hadn't been exaggerating as they strode down a cart path through what seemed like acres of flowers.

When they'd gotten out of the car, he'd taken her hand as if it was the most natural thing in the world. With her fingers laced with his, she gave their joined hands a little swing.

"This is gorgeous, Josiah." She looked up at him, so solid and so very handsome in the midday sun. "I'm glad you brought me here. It's as if we're the only people on earth."

A slight smile tipped the corners of his lips. "I've never known anyone quite like you, Sophie."

"My father says I'm one of a kind." She laughed. "I think it's a compliment."

He turned to face her, and the look in his blue eyes had her heart skipping several beats. "It's definitely one."

When they'd reached the field, he'd removed his jacket and pushed up the sleeves of his shirt. His forearms were strong and sprinkled with a light dusting of hair. The smell of sandalwood and a familiar warm male scent made something tighten low in her abdomen.

His blue eyes darkened, and when he tucked a stray dark curl behind her ear, his gaze never leaving her face, she could tell he wanted to kiss her. She knew that as surely as she knew her own name. This time, there would be no lookie-loos on the shore or in another boat to worry about.

They were alone here, just the two of them under a cloudless sky, surrounded by the sweet scent of wildflowers in full bloom.

"I don't want to presume." His voice was a husky rumble as he stepped closer.

Slipping her hand from his, Sophie placed her hands on his shoulders and smiled up at his too-serious expression. "If you're asking for permission to kiss me, the answer is yes."

The permission had barely left her lips when his mouth closed over hers, his lips exquisitely gentle and achingly tender.

Though she sensed the pent-up need in him—or perhaps that was only her own urges—the kiss started out slowly, as if they had all the time in the world.

Josiah pressed his lips to hers time and time again, each gentle caress sending shivers of delight coursing up her spine.

His hands rested lightly on her hips as they continued to kiss. Though she knew it wasn't possible, Sophie swore the heat of his touch burned all the way through to her skin.

When his tongue swept her lips, she opened to him, relishing the feel of his tongue against hers as he kissed her with a slow thoroughness that left her weak and trembling.

Her blood felt as if it were on fire as desire coursed through her veins. She twined her fingers in his thick dark hair and pressed herself against him.

She longed to run her hands over his body, to feel the coiled strength of skin and muscle sliding under her fingers.

As they continued to kiss, her hat tumbled to the ground. Still, they kissed.

This, Sophie thought, this fire, this connection, was what she had been waiting for her entire life. It wasn't simply that Josiah knew how to kiss, it was the deep connection she felt for him that made kissing him so powerful.

She wasn't simply kissing just anyone, she was kissing Josiah. This man who cared deeply about so many things. This man who'd stopped to help a stranger, who'd bought a Coca-Cola and who'd taken her for a ride in his Tin Lizzie.

She wanted to never let him go.

She arched back, giving him full access to her neck, where he planted kisses along the underside of her jaw. While he did that, his hands slid up her sides, stopping just below her breasts, which strained against the thin fabric, eager for his touch.

The kisses and light touch had a moan coming from her lips. "My sweet Josiah. I—"

Without warning, he broke away, stepping back, his breath coming in fast puffs. He leaned over, bracing his hands against his thighs as if he'd just run a long race and was fighting for breath.

Standing there, dazed and trembling, Sophie understood. She was having difficulty catching her own breath. More, she was having difficulty quelching the desire that had her blood running hot.

She'd seen the fire in Josiah's eyes and understood that him pulling back had nothing to do with a lack of desire for her.

Sophie wanted to tell him this was a dream, and they could do whatever they wanted in it, but she remained silent.

"I apologize profusely for taking such liberties." He raked a hand through his hair. "I have never before lost control in such a manner."

His response was so honest and befuddled, it brought a slight smile to her lips.

"I wanted to kiss you as much as you wanted to kiss me."

Despite herself, her voice shook when she added, "There's something between us, Josiah."

"I can't do this." He whirled and strode back down the path in the direction they'd come.

Reaching over, Sophie slowly picked up her hat and dusted it off.

Just as abruptly as he'd stridden off, Josiah turned and stalked back, misery on his face.

Sophie wanted to step to him, wrap her arms around him and hold him tight. Though she didn't take her eyes off him, something had her remaining in place.

"When Daisy died, the grief from her passing was more than I could bear." Josiah spoke slowly, as if trying to rein in rioting thoughts. "I vowed I would never open my heart to anyone ever again. I could not, would not, risk the pain of losing someone I loved ever again."

Sophie's breath caught, then began again. She nodded, sensing he had more to say.

"Now, today, with you—"

"They were kisses," Sophie told him, yearning to ease his pain. "Nothing more."

"Are you saying you don't feel anything for me?"

She wouldn't lie to him. Couldn't lie to him.

"I do feel something for you." She spoke softly. "But I don't want you to feel guilty about kissing me."

"I don't want to feel what I do for you."

"Josiah, it's not your fault. Don't you know?" She offered a quick smile, opting to be lighthearted. "I'm simply irresistible."

Startled for a moment, he only stared. Then a chuckle came from deep within him and turned into a full-fledged laugh.

She started laughing, too, and the tense moment disappeared.

Tempted to embrace him, Sophie wrapped her arms around

herself instead. "Forget about the kisses. Tell me what else you have planned for us today."

THOUGH SOPHIE MADE A DETERMINED EFFORT, forgetting about the kisses wasn't that easy. Not when the man who'd had her blood flowing hot sat only a few feet away.

Still, on the return trip to the fairgrounds, Sophie tried her best. She knew Josiah tried, too, despite the frequent looks he slanted at her mouth every few minutes.

The drive went quickly. Too quickly, Sophie thought. Once they were at the fairgrounds, they would be surrounded by people. She liked it best when it was just her and Josiah.

She shifted slightly in her seat as the scenery whizzed by. "I didn't think these cars could go this fast."

Josiah smiled. "Thirty miles per hour is a good cruising speed, but when I go to visit my family in Baltimore, it can easily hold a speed of forty-five."

Sophie nodded. She'd seen the historical markers and knew he referred to the Baltimore and GraceTown Turnpike built in 1807. This well-maintained road of crushed stone had been a forerunner of modern turnpikes. "Do you see your family often?"

"Weekly," he acknowledged. "Sometimes more."

"I see my parents every day." Sophie smiled. "We're very close."

"That speaks well of them."

"I don't understand."

"Having such a caring daughter, one who enjoys spending time with them, tells me they were good to you as you grew to womanhood."

Sophie nodded.

"I wonder what such good parents would think of a man who took their daughter riding in the countryside without their permission or a chaperone."

Though the question might have been spoken in a light-hearted tone, there was an undercurrent of something more.

"I told you they trust my judgment." Suddenly, it struck her. "Do you see something wrong in my actions?"

He didn't answer for several long seconds. "No, but there are some who would. And who would see mine as highly improper as well."

Sophie considered. This was her dream, and in it, she didn't care what anyone thought. She was determined to enjoy every second of these moments with Josiah.

"I guess that's their issue." She waved a dismissive hand. "I'm enjoying this time with you too much to care what anyone thinks."

Josiah's smile had the tight set to his jaw easing and the light returning to his eyes.

Glancing out the side of the vehicle, Sophie thought she saw a house, but then she blinked, and it was gone.

"Do you know that some people believe GraceTown abounds in paranormal activity, ah, events where no satisfactory explanation is available?"

By his raised eyebrow as he slanted a glance in her direction, the comment had surprised him.

She could understand. The change of topic had surprised her as well. Her goal had been to get his thoughts off other people's reactions to their behavior. To her way of thinking, there was no way either of them could fully enjoy their time together if they were worried about what other people thought.

"I have heard some describe unexplainable happenings." Josiah spoke slowly, as if trying to form the words in his mind before saying them. "The minister even spoke of it from the pulpit several weeks ago."

"You're kidding."

"I am not," he said earnestly.

"What did he say?" As Sophie had grown up in GraceTown, she'd heard what her parents labeled ghost stories. But the thought of any member of the clergy addressing the rumors brought a smile to her face.

"Oh, he was quite serious about belief in such things being the work of Satan."

"We're all entitled to our opinion," she said with a breezy sigh.

"What is your opinion, Sophie?"

If he hadn't appeared genuinely interested, she might have made some flippant remark and changed the subject...again. But she enjoyed their conversations and wouldn't even mind a debate or two.

"I believe there are many things in this world that can't be explained away by blaming them on the devil." She smiled and shrugged. "We humans can't begin to comprehend the complexity of all that is out there."

"But why GraceTown?" Genuine puzzlement filled Josiah's voice. "Why not Baltimore? Or some other town?"

"I don't know." Sophie lifted her shoulders and let them drop. "I don't think anyone knows."

"You're saying that you believe...what exactly? That it's possible to see and speak with people who have died?"

She nodded.

"Do you think it's possible, then, to travel back in time, like the Time Traveller in Mr. HG Wells's story?"

Sophie had read *The Time Machine* a long time ago, and the concept had intrigued her. Her breath caught in her throat.

Could it be that this wasn't simply a pleasant dream that she would soon awake from? Could she have somehow traveled back in time?

A warm hand closed over her arm. "Sophie."

Sophie realized they'd pulled into the same lot where the Model T had been parked before. Concern blanketed Josiah's face.

"I didn't mean to upset you by suggesting such preposterous things." His voice dropped to a soothing whisper. "I was being ridiculous."

"No." She placed her hand atop his and gazed into his eyes. "It's just that what you said struck me as a definite possibility."

ONCE THEY STEPPED from the car, there was no more talk of paranormal activity, unexplained happenings or time travel. Sophie forced the fear from her body. She was having the best day she could recall, and she would not spoil it with unnecessary speculation.

"Would you care to share a meal with me?" Josiah gestured to an area where men, women and children sat on benches at long tables covered in red-and-white-checked oilcloth.

Sophie's stomach growled at the thought of food. Only now did she remember that the last time she'd eaten had been hours ago. "I would love to share a meal with you."

"Good." As they walked, Josiah reached over, then held out part of a wildflower that must have gotten caught in the brim of her hat.

"Oops," she said and experienced a twinge of regret as he tossed it to the ground.

Once they'd gotten their food, Sophie resisted the urge to sit too close to Josiah, conscious of the curious glances tossed their way, as they dined on a delicious meal of grilled clams and mussels with potatoes, corn and sausage.

"I think this has to be the most delicious food I've eaten in a long time." Studying the last mussel on her plate, Sophie decided it would be a shame to waste it. She stabbed it with her fork and popped it into her mouth.

"You cleaned your plate." Josiah leaned back on the bench, his lazy gaze perusing her even as a smile lifted his lips.

"I did." As the look of masculine appreciation in his eyes fired her senses, she liked knowing she could be herself around him, that they could have a good time simply by sharing a meal together.

They'd spoken primarily of family over the meal, sharing little anecdotes and stories that had them both chuckling. The time had gone so fast that Sophie realized she hadn't had a chance to ask him about the other speakers he'd mentioned wanting to see today.

"I know you said you wanted to hear Mr. Bryan and Lucy Branham speak, but was there someone else you wanted to hear today?"

"Before Mr. Bryan took the stage, I listened to Dr. Edward Amherst Ott of Chicago. He spoke on community building."

"That sounds interesting." Pushing her empty plate to the side, Sophie leaned forward, giving Josiah her full attention. "Community development has always been a special interest of mine."

"Really?"

Sophie frowned at the surprise in his voice. "Do you think I wouldn't be interested because I'm a woman?"

Despite her best efforts, her voice rose before she could remind herself that even if Josiah did feel that way, this was a time when women's roles in society were very different. Not only couldn't they vote, but their function was restricted primarily to homemaking.

"No. Not because of that, other than you are the only woman of my acquaintance to express such interest." He shot her a sheepish smile. "Not that I know many women, other than my mother and sisters. Even among my male acquaintances, I am the only one interested in such matters."

Sophie relaxed. "If you had been speaking today instead of Dr. Ott, what would you have said? What kind of changes do you want for GraceTown?"

Josiah appeared pleased by the question. "I believe a more educated workforce is a better workforce. I'd like to see the community focus more on helping younger people to obtain a high school education. I'd also like to see more respect for shopgirls."

"Shopgirls." Sophie pulled her brows together. "Women who work in shops, like me?"

Shifting uncomfortably, Josiah nodded. "Many, or rather, there are some who feel that women who take jobs in high-class department stores where men of means like to shop are of questionable virtue."

It took everything in Sophie not to laugh out loud. "You mean everyone thinks they're trying to land a wealthy husband."

"Yes."

"Some probably are," Sophie conceded. "I'm sure the majority are simply trying to earn enough money to get by. It wasn't easy... I mean, it's not easy for a single woman in a society that values marriage."

"No," he agreed. "It isn't." He studied her for a long moment. "Have you ever considered matrimony?"

"There has never been anyone in my life who's tempted me to take that walk down the aisle," she told him quite seriously. "Do I want to get married? Yes, if I find the right man."

"What kind of man would he need to be?"

"Intelligent, kind and with a good sense of humor." Sophie and Ruby had discussed this many times. "He wouldn't need to be drop-dead gorgeous, but he would have to be someone who appeals to me on a physical level. I want a man who likes children and pets and who sees me as an equal."

She'd run out of breath and decided that was a good place to stop.

"You appear to have given this matter much thought."

"When you're my age and many of your friends are married, some with children, you look at their lives and think how you would like your own to look." She cocked her head. "How long were you and Daisy married?"

"Four years."

"You said you weren't blessed with children." She kept her tone casual. "Had you decided to wait until your career was more established?"

Surprise flickered across his handsome face, as if that had never been a consideration. "No," he said quite simply. "My wife had a delicate constitution."

Whatever that meant, Sophie thought. "I imagine that was difficult for both of you."

"It was." He blew out a breath. "You know, most say it had to be hard on Daisy, and it was, but they never seem to think that having a family was also my dream, not simply hers."

"I'm sorry that didn't happen."

"I tell myself that with Daisy passing so young it was for the best. A child should grow up with a mother."

"There isn't a single doubt in my mind that you would have been able to cope admirably."

Josiah gave a nod, then his expression brightened. "It sounds as if the Emerson Quartet is tuning up."

"I don't believe I've heard of them."

"They are one of the most popular musical acts on the Chautauqua schedule." Josiah flashed a smile. "Would you like to watch their performance?"

Sophie wasn't sure how much longer this dream would last —if it was a dream, that was. Until she woke up, she would seize every moment. She stood and gestured to the tent. "If we want a seat, we'd best get going."

7

Josiah resisted the urge to take Sophie's hand. He'd liked the way it had felt in his, so small and soft, when he had helped her out of the rowboat. Which was funny, considering how tough she was inside.

She had a quick mind, one of the quickest he'd encountered. Speaking with her over dinner had been like talking business with a colleague.

Daisy had been intelligent, but her focus had been on being a homemaker. She'd done an excellent job and had always been interested in what he'd had to say. When he'd brought up business issues or concerns, she'd always listened intently and made supportive comments.

They'd had a good marriage. He'd been happy and content.

He slanted a sideways glance at Sophie. Each time his parents or sisters brought up him marrying again, he shut them down. Josiah told them that he didn't believe he would ever marry again. He told them his heart belonged to Daisy.

That hadn't been the entire story, though. When Daisy had passed, the grief had been overwhelming. The thought of opening his heart to another, and possibly losing her, too, and facing that grief all over again had felt like more than he could handle.

Josiah had concluded his focus would be on his work and on being the best uncle he could be to his sisters' children.

Now he wondered if he'd been too quick to cast aside the possibility of another wife.

Catching him staring, Sophie smiled. She really did have a lovely smile that lit up her entire face. The color on her lips was gone, taken away by the kisses they'd shared.

An elbow in his side brought him quickly back to reality.

"There are two seats in the back row over there." Sophie spoke in a low tone. "What do you think?"

"Yes. Those will work quite nicely." Josiah placed a light hand on her back as they made their way to the chairs. Despite his decision to be circumspect in public, it was more difficult than he'd imagined to be this close to her and not touch her.

When he thought of the kisses they'd shared in the field of wildflowers, he wanted to touch more than her back or her arm. Under the cloudless blue sky with the sun shining hot overhead and the sweet smell of blooming flowers in the air, he'd felt the coldness inside him begin to thaw.

The ice that surrounded his heart, the ice that he thought would always be there, had cracked just a little.

Sophie smiled at the woman sitting on her other side while he took a seat on the aisle beside her.

"Tell me again who we're listening to."

Sophie might have directed the question to Josiah, but the matronly woman to her right answered.

"They're called the Emersons." The woman's voice shook with excitement. "My sister, who lives in Vermont, saw them at the Chautauqua in Northfield. She said they are amazing."

"I can't wait to hear them," Sophie told the woman, then returned her focus to Josiah. "This should be good."

The quartet, four boys dressed in short pants, suspenders and sporting bow ties, offered the audience bright smiles.

A man who had to be their father, given his age and resemblance to the boys, stepped to the microphone.

"Welcome, one and all. My name is George Emerson." The man gestured to the boys. "These are my four sons—Roy, Louis, Carl and Ralph."

The boys waved, and the audience applauded.

Once the clapping settled down, George offered a warm smile. "If your family is like mine, some of our most treasured memories are of gathering around a piano or organ for sing-alongs. Tonight, my four sons will be singing several popular songs for you that I'm sure you will all know. If the words are familiar, I'd encourage you to join in on the chorus. If they aren't familiar, I believe you'll quickly learn them."

Laughter rippled around the tent.

At a signal from their father, the boys launched into "Ida, Sweet as Apple Cider," followed immediately by "In the Shade of the Old Apple Tree."

Josiah knew the words to both songs, but he sensed the tunes were new to Sophie. Surprisingly, he found himself wanting to sing along with the others. Some sang with great gusto. Others sang off-key, some of them making up for their lack of prowess with enthusiasm.

By the time the boys got to the second chorus of "In the Shade of the Old Apple Tree," Sophie joined in. Josiah added his voice to hers, not surprised when they harmonized beautifully.

He couldn't keep from grinning, unable to recall the last time he'd had such a pleasurable afternoon.

"Sweet Adeline" followed, and it quickly became apparent that it was a crowd favorite.

This time, he and Sophie, along with everyone else in the

tent, belted out the chorus. Somehow, as they were singing and exchanging smiles, her hand wrapped around his arm.

The quartet immediately launched into "In the Good Ol' Summertime." Josiah recalled hearing that the popular song's sheet music had sold a million copies.

The crowd applauded, and whistles and stomping feet filled the tent at the conclusion of the program.

George returned to the microphone. "Thank you for the warm response. You've been such an appreciative audience that, if you would indulge us, we'd like to do one more song."

The roar that went up had Josiah hoping it was a song that Sophie loved. He wanted more than anything for this day to be as special for her as it was for him.

When the boys launched into "By the Light of the Silvery Moon," Sophie smiled broadly, and Josiah knew his prayer had been answered.

When the boys reached the first chorus, the audience locked arms and began to sway as they sang.

Josiah and Daisy had attended a theater production at the Hippodrome theater in Baltimore shortly after it had opened. There had been, for wont of a better word, magic in the air. The vaudeville performers had delivered an outstanding performance, and the atmosphere in the theater had been electric. He'd never experienced anything close to that until now.

By the time the last word was sung and the boys took their bows, happiness slid like melted butter through Josiah's veins.

Sophie turned to the woman beside her.

"It was nice meeting you." Sophie smiled warmly, making no attempt to exit the aisle. "Please write and tell your sister that she was correct. This quartet is well worth seeing."

"I will." The woman's gaze shifted to Josiah. "You and your husband have a lovely evening."

Before more could be said, Josiah stepped into the aisle and held out a hand to Sophie.

Sophie took Josiah's arm as they maneuvered their way through the crowds. They'd gone only a few feet when Josiah was hailed by two men about his age.

"You're just the man we were looking for." The blond man in a brown suit and Panama hat cast a curious glance at Sophie before refocusing on Josiah.

The other man, the buttons of his three-piece suit straining against his girth, didn't even bother glancing in her direction.

"Jasper here," the portly one gestured to his companion, "says you can get us a Tin Lizzie quicker than ordering it directly from the factory."

Josiah turned to Sophie. Though he didn't say a word, she saw the question in his eyes and offered a supportive smile. "I'll leave you men to talk business. I have something I want to ask the woman who was seated next to me."

But when she turned, the woman had disappeared into the crowd. After a moment's hesitation, Sophie headed in the direction of a stand selling sarsaparillas. She'd heard of the drink that had been especially popular in the early twentieth century, but had never tried one. She figured this was as good a time as any.

She never reached the stand. Halfway there, she spotted a Dalmatian puppy cowering against a small tool shed. It couldn't have been more than six weeks old, its eyes shifting back and forth as people strolled by, not paying it any mind.

Changing direction, Sophie strode over. She'd nearly gotten to it when a large crack sounded, and the pup bolted. Sophie reached for the pup, but it ran full bore toward a nearby shed.

The door must have been left slightly ajar, because the puppy easily nosed it open and rushed inside.

Without thinking, Sophie followed.

Instead of finding darkness inside, it took her a second to realize that she was not in a shed, but standing in bright sunlight.

8

That evening, Sophie considered calling her parents to tell them she couldn't make it to dinner. It seemed that the meal she'd eaten with Josiah in her dream had filled her up, and she felt strangely unsettled.

Then she recalled talking about how Dylan sometimes bailed on their plans at the last minute.

An hour later, sitting at the dining room table with her father on one side, her mother on the other, and their cockapoo, Bentley, gnawing on a bully stick at her feet, Sophie felt herself steady.

This was familiar.

"I had the strangest dream." Although Sophie wasn't at all hungry, she added a small dab of couscous to her plate alongside the tiny piece of broiled fish.

Ever since her father's stroke, healthy eating had become a way of life in the Jessup household.

Her mother's eyes brightened. "What was it about?"

Kristin Jessup, a semiretired clinical psychologist, used the psychodynamic approach, which emphasized the role of the unconscious, in her practice.

Sophie's father, a former high school science teacher, leaned forward, ignoring the food on his plate. "You're in for it now. You know your mother has a thing about dreams and their meaning."

Despite the teasing words, Ned Jessup, a balding man in his early seventies with a perpetual smile on his face, appeared as interested as his wife.

"I know she does. That's why I mentioned it." Sophie took a sip of wine. "I'd like to know what she thinks this one means. It felt incredibly real."

In fact, Sophie was having a hard time convincing herself that her time with Josiah had been just a dream.

If it had been, wouldn't she have awakened in her bed?

If she'd passed out at the fairgrounds, wouldn't she have regained consciousness surrounded by medical personnel?

Instead, she'd found herself standing in the space where the third tent had been in the past. And while she'd spent hours with Josiah, only minutes had passed since she'd first entered that third tent.

After finishing her volunteer shift, she'd headed home to change.

Sophie admitted, but only to herself, that she was scared. What had happened to her? Had she been hallucinating? Surely, she hadn't really been transported back to 1916.

"Sweetheart," her mom prompted. "What was the dream?"

Feeling foolish for even entertaining the thought of time travel, Sophie hesitated, wishing in that instant that she'd stayed silent.

It was too late now. Her mother's warm brown eyes were fixed on her, and Sophie had to give her something.

"It was about a man. I mean, in the dream, I met this man. His name was Josiah, and he was wonderful. He was the kind of guy I've always hoped to meet." Just the thought of the time she'd spent with Josiah had warmth flooding her body. "We were together at the fairgrounds, only it was in 1916, not present day. There were Model T cars and horses and buggies."

Sophie's mother nodded. "Was there a sexual component to your dream?"

Heat rose up Sophie's neck. How could she have forgotten her mom was a Freud fangirl?

Sophie cast a quick glance at her dad, who was intently cutting an asparagus spear with a precision once reserved for dissecting frogs.

"Mom, no. We weren't *together* together. We were spending the day together. Like on a date."

"A date that was heading toward..."

Sophie could feel the redness flushing her cheeks. The last thing she wanted to talk about with her parents was her sex life, real or imagined. "We were on a simple date. No *toward*."

Her mother arched a brow.

"Josiah and I didn't have sex."

How was it that simply saying the words had her blushing like a fifteen-year-old?

"I had to ask." Her mother offered a benign smile. "Sex is a common theme in dreams."

Sophie could see why her mother was such an effective psychotherapist. There was no censure in her gaze, and Sophie knew, in her heart, no matter how she'd responded, her mother wouldn't have judged. "Well, sadly, there was no sex in this one."

"Darn." Her mother chuckled and took a sip of wine. "Why don't you tell me what did happen?"

"The dream started out at the fairgrounds, only it was 1916." Sophie didn't like getting overly specific when relaying a story. Doing so reminded her of her mother's brother Tom, who gave too many details when telling a story or joke.

Still, Sophie knew from past experience that small details

were not only important in dream analysis, but also essential for an accurate interpretation.

"A man—he introduced himself as Josiah Huston—asked if I was okay." Sophie's lips curved as she remembered the concern on his face.

Her mother's calm gaze never wavered. "Why did he ask you that?"

"I believe he sensed I was overwhelmed and scared." Sophie responded as if she were giving a report. "I was. I couldn't figure out how I'd gotten there."

"In 1916?"

"Yes," Sophie admitted, then added, "Even though I kept telling myself it was a dream, being there felt incredibly real. So real it frightened me."

"It sounds as if you experienced what is called a vivid dream. These kinds of dreams feel very real."

"What causes them?"

"A variety of factors." Her mother's tone turned reassuring. "What I recommend doing, and what it sounds like you actually already did, is to practice lucid dreaming. It's the art of knowing you are inside a dream while you're dreaming."

"Lucid dreaming." Sophie rolled the words around on her tongue.

"The clients that I have who've experienced vivid dreams and practice lucid dreaming also find it helpful to keep a record of all that you remember. Either write it down or use a voice recorder. Those kinds of detailed records can help you recognize more easily that you're dreaming."

"I can do that," Sophie agreed.

"Tell me more about this dream." Ignoring the food still on her plate, her mother gave Sophie her complete attention. "How did you respond to this man's approach?"

"I went with him, and he bought me a Coke." Sophie smiled.

The bottle had felt so cold in her hand, and the Coke had tasted really good.

Surprise skittered across her mother's face. "Did they even have Coke in 1916?"

"They'd just introduced the iconic glass bottle around then, though I don't think they'd started using the nickname Coke yet." Sophie scooped up some couscous, discovering that unburdening herself had stimulated her appetite. "I felt steadier after drinking the Coke. We started talking cars, and Josiah took me for a ride in his Model T. We drove to Culler Lake, went for a rowboat ride, then we went for a walk through a field of wildflowers. After that, he brought me back to the fairgrounds. I can't recall a lovelier day."

"Did he mention what he did for a living?"

"Is that important?"

"At this point, it's impossible to know what is relevant and what isn't."

"He ran a Ford dealership."

"Interesting." Her mother tapped a finger against her lips. "Any idea how old he was?"

"My age," Sophie told her mom.

Kristin arched a brow. "And he wasn't married?"

Sophie set down the wineglass she'd just picked up and laughed. "I'm not either, Mom."

"You don't live in 1916. Then, most men—and women—were married long before their thirtieth birthday."

"His wife died the year before from infection when her appendix ruptured."

Kristin's gaze grew thoughtful. "This was a very detailed dream."

"It felt incredibly real." Sophie gave a little laugh, embarrassed by the surge of emotion. "When we were walking through the wildflowers, he kissed me. Or maybe I kissed him first."

A look Sophie couldn't decipher filled her mother's eyes. "You were attracted to him."

It was a statement, not a question.

"I am." Sophie flushed. "I mean, I was. In the dream, there was an intense attraction. One, I believe, that went both ways. Simply being with him made me happy."

Her mother nodded.

"The only disturbing part was that it all happened in 1916."

"Finding yourself in a new room or place is a common dream theme. It's also not unusual for a person to feel like they've discovered a magical door to another world."

"Really?" Sophie didn't know whether to be excited or disappointed. Out of the corner of her eye, she saw her dad, fork in hand, gazing at her with a curious look.

"Really." Kristin smiled. "I tell my clients to view these dreams as a type of self-discovery where you learn something about yourself. Do you have any idea what this person in your imagination represents? Does the connection you felt with him in your dream offer insight into what's happening in your current life?"

"I'm still trying to process the fact that it seemed so real." Sophie lifted her hands, then let them drop. "Do you have any thoughts?"

"I would only be speculating."

Sophie circled a hand in the air, impatient for her mother to continue. "Speculate away. I won't hold you to it."

Her mother chuckled. "First, why don't you tell me how your feelings for this Josiah compare to what you feel for Dylan?"

"I like Dylan. He's fun to be around, and he's nice. Our relationship is...comfortable." Sophie paused. "The connection with Josiah was completely different."

"Keep in mind that I'm speculating..." Her mom held up a

hand, palm out. "It seems as if your subconscious may have given you a glimpse of what true love would feel like."

"Dylan and I, well, we've never talked about love. We've been happy with the way things are between us."

"You've been *comfortable* with the way things are."

Sophie waved an airy hand. "Same thing."

"Not at all. Your dream experience with Josiah should tell you that."

Sophie remained silent.

"You've been dating Dylan for nearly two years." Her mother spoke in a conversational tone. "Why continue to see him if the feelings aren't there?"

It was a question Sophie had asked herself many times, especially over the last couple of months.

"Like I said, we have fun," Sophie said, then qualified, "Most of the time, anyway. Having a boyfriend to do things with doesn't suck."

Her dad snorted out a laugh.

Her mother shot him a glinting glance before refocusing on Sophie. "I recall you mentioning he also volunteered to help at the Chautauqua today. How did that go?"

Until this moment, Sophie had forgotten all about that. "It didn't. Something came up."

"He didn't show?" Her mother managed to keep any censure from her voice, but her gaze turned sharp and assessing.

"He called and canceled."

"You were disappointed."

Sophie lifted one shoulder, then let it drop. "It was his choice."

"You were disappointed." For whatever reason, her mom would not let it drop.

Sophie sighed.

With her mother's steady gaze on her, she couldn't lie. Not to

who didn't even exist. She pulled herself back to the present when she realized her father had continued to speak.

"Your happiness is what matters most to us, Sophie." Her father's intense gaze never left her face. "Let that knowledge guide whatever decisions you make going forward."

9

On Friday, Sophie rose early and dressed carefully for the day in a green silk dress trimmed in lace. She told herself that the extra time she spent with her hair wasn't because she expected to see Josiah. She simply wanted to look her best while volunteering.

Though she'd tried to convince herself that what she'd experienced yesterday had been some kind of dream, she couldn't make herself believe it. The only other explanation—and this was about as farfetched as it got—was that she'd traveled through time. But how? And more important, could she do it again?

Eyeing the love token sitting on her nightstand, Sophie decided to take it with her to the fairgrounds. Logic told her the coin had no special powers, but it *had* been with her yesterday when she'd seen the third tent.

At the fairgrounds administrative offices, Sophie checked in for her volunteer shift. Though she was eager to make a beeline to the tents, instead of rushing out the door, she went looking for Alcidean.

She found her in the storage room, intently searching

through a stack of boxes.

Sophie cleared her throat.

Straightening from the box in front of her, Alcidean turned. A smile lifted her lips. "Sophie. What can I help you with?"

"I can see that you're busy—"

"Understatement." The woman laughed. "There has been a bigger response than we imagined to the Chautauqua performances. I'm not complaining. It's a good problem to have."

"Is that why you put up a third tent?" Sophie blurted, seizing the opening.

"Third tent?" Alcidean chuckled and shook her head. "Two tents are all we can handle."

"What about the one by the—?" Seeing Alcidean's puzzlement, Sophie stopped and backpedaled. "I simply thought you might be considering erecting a third one in anticipation of higher attendance this weekend."

"Nope. Besides, we only have enough performers for two tents. And enough volunteers." Alcidean glanced at her watch. "Isn't your shift—?"

"I'm heading there now." Sophie paused. "Before I go, is there anything I can help you find?"

"I'm good." Alcidean made a shooing motion. "Enjoy your day, and thanks again for volunteering."

Sophie smiled, thinking of Josiah. "It's been a pleasure."

Alcidean nodded. "I always say that volunteers get more out of the experience than they put in. Not everyone agrees with that, but I've seen it time and time again."

"Count me as a believer."

Once she left the administration building, Sophie set off in the direction of the tents. Her heart rate picked up speed with each step. The rapid beating came to an abrupt halt when she saw only two tents.

For a long moment, Sophie stared at the space where the third tent had sat yesterday, trying to will it to appear. Nothing.

Swallowing her disappointment, Sophie strode into the first tent. At a quick glance, she estimated it to be half full. Though very few in the audience had chosen to dress in period garb, everyone seemed to be in a fine mood.

On the makeshift stage, a man wearing a bowler hat, a brown jacket, taupe pants and a pink silk shirt regaled the audience with vocal selections from the Italian opera *The Barber of Seville.*

She noticed ice and water filled his pitcher to the brim. The fans were perfectly positioned. As everything appeared in order, she slipped out and moved to the next tent.

Inside, a group of thespians from Collister College offered a production of the Shakespeare comedy *Much Ado About Nothing.* Though there was minimal scenery, the crowd's enthusiastic response to the performance buoyed Sophie's flagging spirts.

She considered staying to watch—the costumes the group had brought with them from the college were amazing—but the tent was already at capacity.

Stepping outside, Sophie found herself once again glancing at where the third tent had stood yesterday.

Nothing but dirt and little tufts of grass marked the spot. She walked around the outside of the other two tents, then back and forth across the ground.

"Yoo-hoo, Sophie."

She looked up and smiled as Bernita Cuthbert, retired real estate broker and lover of antiques, hurried toward her. Bernita had always been one of Sophie's favorite customers. Her bright purple dress, complete with a matching hat topped with a massive white feather, suited her larger-than-life personality.

"Are you volunteering today, too?"

"I am." Bernita gestured with one hand toward a metal

Quonset. "That's where the performers wait for their turn. Having the opportunity to chat with such talent is a difficult job, but I'm rising to the challenge."

Sophie laughed. "I have no doubt."

Bernita inclined her head. "Were you searching for something when I walked up?"

Ignoring the sick feeling in the pit of her stomach, Sophie said, "Nothing important."

How could she tell the woman she was searching for a tent that apparently only she could see? She could only imagine the look on Bernita's face if she added that she'd brought a love token with her because she suspected it had magical properties.

"Well, I'd better get back. My break is nearly over." As Bernita hurried off, she called over her shoulder, "That's a darling purse."

Once Bernita was out of sight, Sophie opened the clasp of the purse with the lace waterfall and removed the love token. Holding it pinched between her fingers, she deliberately read the inscription aloud. "Love Be Yours, Love Be Mine."

When no tent appeared, she squeezed her eyes tightly shut and concentrated on the coin. *Take me back to Josiah.*

She opened her eyes. Still no tent. Disappointment flooded her. It was becoming obvious that the coin didn't possess any special powers.

Still, she slipped it into the pocket of her dress, gaining odd comfort from having it close. The sound of a barking dog, reminding her of the puppy she'd seen yesterday, had her turning.

And there it was. The third tent.

Sounds of raucous laughter rolled through the open flaps.

Sophie's heart slammed against her rib cage, and her breath caught in her throat. Like she was sleepwalking, she moved toward the tent, her heart beating so hard it nearly drowned out the sounds coming from inside.

Taking a deep, steadying breath, Sophie stepped through the flaps. Like yesterday, everyone in the tent was dressed in period garb. This time, instead of Mr. Bryan orating from the stage, a two-person vaudeville act performed.

The sign on the easel indicated they were known as Coates and Gilbert. The man, in crazy makeup and playing up his large girth, had laughter rolling from the audience, while the pretty woman, in her role as the straight half of the duo, had an excellent poker face and an even better singing voice.

Based on the crowd's enthusiastic response, their slapstick humor and antics were hitting a chord.

Sophie barely spared them a glance. Her gaze quickly found the exit she'd used yesterday. Instead of heading right to it, she turned and stepped out the way she'd come in.

There was no shock at seeing Tin Lizzies and horses, only a mind-numbing sense of relief. It appeared it didn't matter which exit or entrance she used. Once she entered the tent, she was in 1916.

She remained where she was for several seconds, using the time to slow her racing heart. She wasn't sure if the fast beat was due to making the transition into this alternate universe or her excitement over the possibility of seeing Josiah again.

Glancing around, she noted men of all shapes and sizes, but no Josiah. Then she chided herself. What were the odds he'd be in this same location at approximately the same time? It wasn't as if they'd set up a time to meet.

Josiah was a busy man. He had a business to run.

Recalling that the fairgrounds was located within walking distance of the GraceTown business district, Sophie smiled and turned in that direction.

THROUGH TRIAL AND ERROR, Josiah had discovered that during the week most customers stopped by the showroom in the afternoons and evenings. That was why Leroy, his best salesman, began his workday at noon.

Since Daisy's death, Josiah had started coming in early and staying late. Most days, anyway. Today, he'd planned to spend the entire day at the fairgrounds, until a photographer from the *Gazette* had asked if he could stop by at ten.

On Tuesday, Josiah had met with Hershel Busbee. The reporter was a gregarious fellow with a knack for ferreting out details that would interest the newspaper's readers. He'd let Josiah know that a photographer would be in touch to set up a time to take photos for the article.

Josiah had been looking forward to attending the Chautauqua and listening to Ben Lindsey, a judge from Denver, give his view on community building. He told himself the change in plans was perhaps for the best.

Going to the fairgrounds would bring up thoughts of Sophie and her abrupt disappearance. He'd shifted away from her for one second to answer a potential customer's question, and when he'd turned back, she was gone.

For the past year, Josiah had told himself he was happy, content even, being alone. He had his family and his work. He didn't need more.

Those few hours he'd spent with Sophie had him rethinking that stance. The door to his heart, which he'd kept firmly shut since Daisy's death, had cracked open, just a little. He'd enjoyed the time with Sophie. He'd hoped, before they parted that evening, they would set a time to meet again.

When Sophie had disappeared without a good-bye, he'd

realized he didn't even know where to begin looking for her. He didn't know where she lived or even where she worked.

Forget her, Josiah told himself. *Concentrate on business.*

He was crouched behind a touring sedan, checking a back tire, when he heard the door open. He rose, thinking the photographer from the *GraceTown Gazette* had arrived.

He stepped out from behind the car to greet the man and inhaled sharply.

Sophie.

The woman he'd been convinced he would never see again stood just inside the door. The dark curls tumbling around her shoulders provided a perfect foil for her emerald-green dress.

"Hello, Josiah." She smiled tentatively. "I hope I'm not interrupting anything."

"Ah..." For once, Josiah's conversational skills deserted him. "This is a surprise."

"I was at the fairgrounds, but you weren't there. I was...disappointed." She brushed a strand of silky hair back from her face with a hand that trembled slightly. "I thought... Well, I thought you might be working, so I decided to stop by in the hopes of seeing you."

"I planned to be at the fairgrounds, but—" Josiah stopped himself from explaining about the photographer. "That isn't important. What's important is that you're here."

They exchanged smiles, and she stepped closer.

"It appears you're working today, but perhaps you'd have time for a break?" A hopeful gleam filled her eyes.

"Actually, I'm waiting for a photographer from—" Josiah paused as the door opened, and a tall, lanky man with a camera around his neck stepped into the showroom.

"Mr. Huston, I'm Merle Watts from the *Gazette*." The man strode across the shiny floor and extended his hand. "I'm sorry if I kept you waiting."

Josiah clasped the man's hand. When Merle cast a curious glance in Sophie's direction, Josiah performed the introductions, adding, "Miss Jessup is a family friend."

Merle dipped his head. "It's a pleasure to meet you, Miss Jessup."

Sophie smiled. "The pleasure is mine, Mr. Watts. I have a keen interest in photography."

"Don't we all?" Mr. Watts turned to Josiah. "Ready to get started?"

"I'd love to observe." Sophie spoke before Josiah had a chance to respond. "If you gentlemen don't object, that is."

"Makes me no nevermind." Merle glanced at Josiah.

"Stay." Relief flooded Josiah. He'd had a vision of her stepping out the door and never returning. "This won't take long."

"Not long at all." Merle flashed a smile at Sophie. "I'm just here to take a few photographs that will run with an article in the *Gazette*."

Sophie's eyes lit up. "What kind of article?"

"The newspaper has been doing a series focusing on successful local businessmen."

Sophie slanted a glance at Josiah, then back at Merle. "You certainly came to the right man."

"Like he said, this shouldn't take long." Josiah met her gaze, trying to will her to see just how much he wanted her to stay.

"Don't rush on my account." Sophie stepped off to the side. "I'll stay out of the way."

"I need to take a few shots to check the lighting first."

"Perhaps Miss Jessup could be in those," Josiah suggested.

Merle shrugged. "If you like."

Josiah held out his hand, which she took.

Merle instructed them to stand close to the touring car, Sophie's hand resting on the shiny black paint of the vehicle.

From there, they moved in front of a wall that displayed the words Huston Ford GraceTown.

The photographer gazed down into his viewfinder, took one picture, then turned the camera on its side and took another.

"The light is definitely better over here." Merle glanced up.

Appearing to understand she'd been dismissed, Sophie moved behind the photographer.

"Mr. Huston, I'd like you to lift your hand now as if you are gesturing to the business name," Merle instructed, his focus on the task at hand.

Merle took a few more shots, changing some controls, then taking more. Then he smiled. "That should do it."

Josiah stepped forward and offered his hand. "I appreciate you coming by."

"I appreciate you making this easy."

"Before you go..." Josiah glanced at Sophie, relieved she showed no signs of bolting. Instead, she was inspecting the inside of the touring car. "Would you have a second to show me how this camera works?"

Sophie stepped closer. "I'm interested as well."

"I'd be delighted to explain what I know." Merle tapped the side of the sharp-edged box, drawing Josiah's eyes from Sophie and back to the camera. "As you probably are aware, over the past three years, we've transitioned from glass plates to sheet film. This particular camera has a reversible reflecting finder. It also has an additional shutter speed for capturing moving objects."

Josiah listened and watched as Merle explained each feature and what it did.

"This uses autographic film, correct?" Josiah asked.

Sophie inclined her head. "What is that?"

"Yes, 116 autographic," Merle confirmed, then turned to

Sophie. "Autographic film allows the photographer to enter his own notes on the negative."

"I hope you realize you do more than take pictures, Mr. Watts. You capture memories." Her smile was so warm it had the tips of Merle's ears turning red. "Thank you for the explanation of how this camera works."

"Yes, I appreciate you taking the time to show us," Josiah echoed. For a second, he was struck by what he'd just said.

Us.

As if he and Sophie were a couple.

Simple semantics, he assured himself. Nothing more. Still, the word had felt right on his tongue.

"It was my pleasure." Merle gestured toward the Model T. "One of these days, I'm going to get me a Tin Lizzie."

"It's a beauty." Josiah easily slipped into business mode. "Let me know when you're ready, and we'll see what we can work out."

"I'll do that," Merle told him, then dipped his head toward Sophie. "Ma'am."

Sophie waited until the door shut behind him to speak.

"Though it wasn't my intention, I believe I embarrassed him."

Josiah arched a brow.

"With my comment about capturing memories." For just a second, her eyes turned dreamy. "I believe in my heart that's what he does. I heard it said once that photographs are memories frozen in time." Then she waved a hand, looking mildly embarrassed herself. "That probably sounds silly."

"I believe he was touched by your words." He took her hand. "I told him I'd like copies of the photos he took of you and me. I will share them with you once they arrive. I rather like the idea of the memory of today being frozen in time."

"I'll never forget our time together," she said fiercely.

"Nor will I." Josiah cleared his throat. "Speaking of time together, if you are available, I'd very much like to spend the day with you."

Surprised pleasure swept across her face. "Don't you have to work?"

He shook his head.

"Well, then, yes, I'm available, and I'd love to spend the day with you."

Relief flooded Josiah as he pushed open the door leading to the back of the building. "I was concerned your parents might order you not to see me again."

"I told them about you. They approve of me spending time with you."

Josiah couldn't hide his shock. "They approve of you consorting with a man who is unknown to them?"

His own mother and father would not take kindly to the thought of one of their daughters meeting a man at the fairgrounds and going off in a motorcar with him.

"They thought you sounded like a nice man and gave me their blessing."

The comment had him blinking in surprise.

"Even though we haven't been properly introduced?" Josiah spoke cautiously, feeling his way over unfamiliar terrain.

Sophie waved an airy hand. "They trust my judgment."

"You're positive they—"

"I also told them about your business and how it's right here in town, so they feel safe knowing you're an upstanding member of the community. And that they can find you if I go missing," Sophie added with a wink. "Besides, I'm hardly a blushing debutante, and my parents know that. They accept the fact that when you have an unmarried daughter nearing thirty, the traditional rules don't apply."

No, Josiah thought, Sophie was definitely not traditional. He considered himself a traditional man, and yet, breaking with tradition to spend time with Sophie made him happy.

"What shall we do this afternoon?" she asked. "That is, if you're certain I'm not interrupting your day. I realize it was presumptuous of me to stop by unannounced when we didn't have plans."

"The only reason we didn't have plans was that you disappeared before we could make any." He offered a smile to show he didn't mean the words as a condemnation. After all, he was the one who'd been waylaid by a customer. "My afternoon is yours. What do you fancy doing?"

"Not the fairgrounds. Something...different." She gazed up at him, the look in those hazel eyes warm and inviting. "Do you have a suggestion?"

Josiah thought for a moment. "What about Funland?"

She hesitated for only a second, then smiled. "I'd love to go there with you."

He wasn't surprised Sophie was familiar with the park on the outskirts of GraceTown. When he'd moved here, his household goods hadn't been unpacked before a number of people had mentioned it to him. "It's likely to be busy, although perhaps not as much as usual because of the Chautauqua performances."

"I don't mind busy," Sophie told him. "Crowds give me an excuse to take your arm."

"You don't need an excuse," he assured her.

When they reached his car, she turned and rested her back against the passenger door. "I've never been to Funland."

"That surprises me." He paused and considered. "If that type of park doesn't interest you, we could—"

"I'm not saying it doesn't interest me," she protested. A soft look filled her eyes. "I believe I was meant to go there for the first time with you."

The thought pleased him.

"I have not been there yet myself," he admitted. "We shall have the pleasure of exploring it for the first time together."

In order to open her door, he was forced to reach around her. Josiah expected Sophie to move, or at least to shift out of the way. Instead, she remained where she was, and his hand brushed the softness of her hip before closing around the handle.

She was so close he could smell the scent of lilacs in her hair and see the darker ring of gold around the hazel in her eyes.

The desire to pull her close and kiss her until they were both breathless rose strong inside him. From the way she looked at him, she felt the same.

He lowered his head, anticipating the feel of her lips on his, the taste of—

A horn honked.

Jerking back, Josiah glanced around, realizing too late that the sound had come from the other end of the alleyway. The driver of the vehicle sounded his horn one more time before pulling onto the street.

"That was—"

"Bad timing." Sophie rose up on tiptoes and kissed him softly on the mouth.

Though Josiah completely agreed, he didn't know what to think when Sophie turned, opened her door and stepped into the car. "I'm ready when you are."

Josiah had never known a woman who could so completely confound him. Still, he found himself smiling as he started the Tin Lizzie and left the alley, turning in the direction of Funland. "I've heard that this particular amusement park is modeled after Steeplechase Park in New York's Coney Island."

"I've been to Coney Island," Sophie announced, as if mentioning she'd driven to the market. "Several times, in fact."

"Did you enjoy your visits?"

"I did. Very much."

"Well, from what everyone has told me, Funland is much like that, only on a smaller scale."

"Nathan's opened a hot dog stand on Coney Island in 1916—ah, this year, I mean. Does Funland serve Nathan's hot dogs?"

"That's what I'm told." Anticipation surged as Josiah envisioned spending the entire day with this fascinating woman.

"I'd say this day is off to an excellent start."

Glancing at Sophie beside him, Josiah couldn't agree more.

10

Sophie had read all about Funland, the park that had opened at the dawn of the twentieth century and been demolished in the 1960s. She'd even sold a few postcards in her store depicting scenes from the park.

Neither the stories nor the postcard images had prepared her for the size and grandeur of Funland.

Sophie pointed toward the figure-eight roller coaster, the tracks reaching to the skies. "How high do you think that is?"

Josiah's gaze went skyward. He smiled. "Very high."

"This place is amazing." Sophie squeezed Josiah's arm. "I know we spoke about getting something to eat, but I'd like to do some exploring first. You know, check things out."

"Whatever you want to do," he told her.

As they talked, they continued to walk. There were people everywhere—women in dresses and hats and men in suits. Even the children were dressed in their Sunday best.

Sophie recalled her parents telling her that when they were first married, they—and everyone they knew—dressed up for not only church, but when they went out for dinner and even when they flew.

"This is a different world," she murmured as she observed a man pull out a pristine white handkerchief from the breast pocket of his suit and hand it to a small boy, who held a dripping ice cream cone.

"Yes, it is." Josiah shook his head. "I've never seen so many attractions in one place."

"It's so beautiful here." Sweet-smelling flowers in bright colors of red, pink and yellow surrounded bushes trimmed in the shapes of mythical creatures.

"It's lovely." His gaze lingered on her. "As are you."

Sophie couldn't stop her smile. "Thank you, kind sir."

Josiah's gaze lingered for a moment longer, then settled on a woman selling paper flowers. "Come with me."

Before Sophie knew what was happening, Josiah grasped her hand, his long strides taking her to the woman's stand.

She was dressed simply in a blue muslin dress, but her matching bonnet was a work of art because of the elaborate flower arrangement.

The woman stopped scanning the crowd and settled her sharp-eyed gaze on Josiah as they approached. "Would you like a flower for your lady? They're very popular."

She held out a gorgeous paper rose, the stem covered in green silk.

Last year, Sophie had had several sprays and wreaths of artificial flowers in her shop. She'd dated them from the Edwardian period, when the creation of handmade flowers had been at its peak.

She wished she could warn the woman it would soon be time to take up a new trade. In her research, Sophie had learned that although artificial flowers had still been extremely popular in 1916, demand for such flowers to decorate dresses, bonnets and hats had dried up after WWI.

"I'd like a wreath of roses to adorn the brim of the lady's hat," Josiah told the woman.

"I have just the thing." The woman reached down, and when she straightened, she held a gorgeous ring of yellow roses. "Will this do?"

Josiah glanced at Sophie.

"It's gorgeous," she said.

"Yes, that will do nicely," he told the woman.

She held out her hand to Sophie. "If you'll give me your hat, miss, I'll be happy to secure these to the brim."

The flowers, so bright and pretty, tempted. But Sophie knew that such quality didn't come cheap. "They are lovely, Josiah, but I can't let you spend so much on me."

"It is but a simple gift. However, if you feel it would be improper, I will understand."

In that moment, Sophie realized if she turned down his gift, he would be disappointed, but he wouldn't sulk or let her refusal to bend to his wishes ruin their day. Not like Dylan sometimes did. But Josiah's feelings would be hurt.

Sophie removed her straw hat and handed it to the lady, then shifted her focus to the man at her side. "Thank you, Josiah."

She wasn't sure how much he paid, but from the woman's delighted expression, it must have been more than she was asking.

Once the flowers were secured to the brim of Sophie's hat, the lady held it out to her.

"Allow me." Josiah lifted it from the woman's hands and smiled at Sophie. With great gentleness, he set the hat on her head, then stepped back and studied her. "Beautiful."

Sophie touched the edge of her hat. "I wish I had a mirror so I could see."

"A moment." Once again, the woman bent over, returning

this time with what Sophie recognized as an art nouveau hand-held mirror. The raised floral design on the back, intricate and striking, extended to the handle.

But Sophie was more interested in seeing her reflection than in admiring the mirror's workmanship and design.

She held it up and gazed at her reflection. The simple straw hat was simple no more. The flowers encircling the brim elevated the hat to a whole different level.

As much as she loved the flowers, it was the thoughtfulness of the man watching her and waiting for her reaction that had her going all gooey inside.

Without giving a thought to where they were, Sophie flung her arms around Josiah and squeezed tight. "I love it. Thank you."

For just a second, he returned the hug, then he stepped back. "You're very welcome."

The happiness that bubbled up inside Sophie filled every inch of her body. She was seized with a sudden urge to skip, something she hadn't done since she'd been a child.

Instead, she strolled with Josiah, arm in arm, taking in the sights and the music from a distant band.

"We're getting closer," Sophie told Josiah, determined to see the band that filled the air with such joyful noise.

"I can hear it." Josiah offered a slight smile. "The music is definitely getting louder."

He'd been such a good sport, she thought, indulging her desire to bypass the other attractions to go in search of the band.

Reaching down, she took his hand and gave it a squeeze. "Thank you."

Puzzlement filled his eyes, while a smile hovered at the corners of his lips. "For what?"

She liked that he laced his fingers with hers instead of releasing her hand.

"For going on this hunt with me."

Confusion furrowed his brow.

"I know it must have seemed silly to you for us to go looking for the source of the music, but—"

"Not silly at all." He surprised her by bringing their joined hands to his lips and placing a kiss on her knuckles. "We wanted to explore the park. That's what we're doing."

He was right. Though they had strolled past most of the rides, they had stopped to watch a mime perform, gotten the flower wreath and enjoyed an ice cream cone, even as the band continued to play.

Often, the rousing melodies would be broken by excited screams and wild laughter.

White lacquered gates sporting an intricate design that spelled out the words Grace Garden drew her eye, even as her ears went on high alert.

Sophie pointed. "The music is coming from in there."

"Good afternoon, sir, ma'am." A Funland employee, resplendent in a fancy blue coat with yellow lapels and cuffs, greeted them with a broad smile, gesturing widely with one arm. "The Garden is through here."

"Is that also where the band is?" Sophie asked.

"Yes, ma'am." The man, with his bushy white eyebrows and walrus mustache of the same color, should have looked ridiculous, but instead, he looked friendly and approachable. He touched the brim of his cap. "Enjoy your visit to Grace Garden."

The moment Sophie stepped through the gate, her breath caught at the surrounding beauty. Thousands of fragrant blooming flowers of every shape and color perfumed the air with their sweet scents.

Still conscious of her quest, Sophie glanced down and spotted the band on a raised platform. Dressed in red coats, white shirts and black bow ties, the eight-member band played their tunes, while the red canopy overhead shielded their heads from the sun.

Concrete benches on each level of the floral terraces were occupied by couples and individuals who applauded after each musical selection. At the base of the platform where the band sat, couples danced.

"I bet there wasn't any dancing when the marches were being played," Sophie told Josiah.

Josiah chuckled. "Probably not."

Since there was no one behind them on the steps leading down to the band, Sophie leaned over and rubbed the velvety soft petals of a fully open red rose between her fingers. Then she inhaled the sweet scent.

When she straightened, she found Josiah staring.

"What's wrong?"

"I was just wondering if I should have asked the woman for a garland of red roses."

Sophie's fingers rose protectively to the edge of her hat. "I love my yellow roses. They're perfect."

An odd look filled his eyes, then he smiled. "The fact that you're happy with your selection pleases me."

The music changed to an infectious beat. Sophie watched as the dancers took four hopping steps sideways, then stopped abruptly, all while raising and lowering their elbows. The strange movements continued.

Sophie pulled her brows together. "What are they doing?"

"The turkey trot." Josiah's lips curved, and his eyes took on a distant glow, almost as if he was looking back. "I'm surprised you don't recognize it. Animal dances were all the rage four, maybe five years ago."

"Ah, yes, the animal dances." Sophie hadn't seen any of the various animal dances, except for the fox-trot, but she remembered reading how President Wilson had canceled his inaugural ball because he'd feared guests would dance the turkey trot.

"Daisy loved them all, especially the grizzly bear and the bunny hug."

"Weren't they considered quite scandalous?"

Sophie hadn't meant anything by the comment, but Josiah's suddenly still shoulders told her he'd taken her words as censure.

"What two married people do in the privacy of their home isn't anyone's business," he said.

"I agree."

"You do?"

Sophie gave a decisive nod. "For the record, I think these dances are great fun." She gestured toward the couples who were smiling and laughing as they flapped their "wings."

"Would you care to dance?" he asked.

Sophie had no clue how to do any of the animal dances, and she really didn't like making a spectacle of herself. Still, she worried a refusal might give him the impression she really had found his and Daisy's behavior scandalous.

"I'd love to dance." After flashing a bright smile, she scurried down the steps. Just as she reached the bottom, the music shifted to a waltz.

Josiah held out his arms.

Sophie stepped to him. As they began to move to the romantic melody, Sophie wished she could press herself tightly against him and rest her head on his broad chest.

He was so strong and so kind. Josiah was the type of man she could put her trust in, one she could depend on, one she could easily love. Not just for a day or a week, but for a lifetime.

These feelings were new, and Sophie hugged them close to her heart. It had never been like this with Dylan. Maybe because she'd never been able to fully rely on him. She'd certainly never seen herself with him in the future.

But how could she and Josiah have a future when he lived in 1916, and she didn't even understand how she'd gotten there?

The thought of losing what she was building with this man had Sophie tightening her hold on his hand and looking up at him. "I don't want this to end."

11

After dancing for several more songs, Sophie and Josiah left Grace Garden and hopped on an open car on the scenic railway that wove its way through Funland.

With a gentle breeze rifling her hair and Josiah's arm resting on the back of the seat, Sophie expelled a happy breath, feeling utterly content.

"What would you like to do next?" he asked, his fingers playing with a lock of her hair.

Sophie considered. "Food?"

Josiah smiled. "I believe I'm ready for some nourishment as well."

"Next stop, picnic area," the conductor, wearing a navy hat with gold letters proclaiming him as such, called out.

"Sounds like where we want to get off," Sophie said.

When the train eased to a stop, Josiah hopped off first, then extended his hand to Sophie.

A gentleman to the core, she thought, as warmth flooded her. She took his hand and didn't let go.

He squeezed her fingers. "What sounds good to you?"

She sniffed the air and immediately caught the scent of hot dogs. "I believe I'd like a hot dog."

"You're easy to please."

She shrugged good-naturedly. "It just sounds good to me."

"To me as well."

They found the Nathan's hot dog stand and, after spending twenty cents for two hot dogs and two Cokes, went in search of a place to sit. They located an empty table on the broad swath of lawn. Some, like them, ate at tables that dotted the vast expanse of grass, while others sat on blankets with picnic baskets open beside them and food spread out before them.

As it had been at Grace Gardens, flowers were everywhere, adding their sweet scent to the air. Instead of eating to music from a band, they were serenaded by the sounds emanating from wind chimes hanging in the trees.

Gazing down at the hot dog she held, topped with mustard, Sophie realized she was hungry. Really hungry.

Out of the corner of her eye, Sophie saw Josiah's eyes widen as she took a big bite of the hot dog, then washed the bite down with a large drink of soda.

"You were hungry." He took a bite of his own hot dog.

She laughed. "What was your first clue?"

Josiah leaned forward, the handkerchief from his pocket in hand. "You've got some mustard right—"

"Josiah. This is a surprise."

For a second, Sophie's gaze locked with Josiah's, then they both turned toward the feminine voice.

Josiah lowered his hand, still holding the handkerchief.

Sophie sat back and offered the woman and man standing beside their table a friendly smile.

The woman wore her golden hair massed in a soft coil a little beyond the crown of her head. Her pale blue dress and matching hat flattered her blond prettiness. The man beside her wore a suit and a big smile.

"Edith. Thaddeus." Josiah pushed back his chair and rose. "This is a nice surprise. It's good to see you both."

"I thought you were meeting with the photographer from the *Gazette* today." The woman might have been speaking to Josiah, but her gaze kept returning to Sophie.

"I met with him this morning. He was a very pleasant fellow." Josiah gestured to the empty chairs at the table. "Please join us, and I'll tell you all about his visit. But first, I need to introduce you to someone."

Having felt awkward sitting when everyone else was standing, Sophie had risen to her feet.

"Miss Sophia Jessup, I would like to introduce you to my sister and brother-in-law, Edith and Thaddeus Holland."

Sophie extended her hand to Edith, who took it and smiled. "It's a pleasure to meet you, Miss Jessup."

Sophie returned her smile, noticing Edith had the same bright blue eyes as her brother. "It's lovely to meet you as well."

She then turned to Thaddeus and was about to extend her hand when she recalled that, while it was acceptable for ladies to shake hands when introduced, they rarely shook hands with men. She inclined her head. "Mr. Holland."

"Please, call me Thaddeus." The man offered a friendly smile.

"I'd love for both of you to call me Sophie."

"Let's sit," Josiah interjected when his sister opened her mouth. "No need to stand. If you are planning to get a hot dog—"

"No," Edith spoke quickly. "We ate earlier. We were passing by when Thaddeus spotted you."

"Then you can join us while we finish our food." Josiah waited for his sister to sit before resuming his seat.

Though Sophie was still hungry, she felt awkward eating while Edith and Thaddeus watched.

Josiah, on the other hand, appeared to show no such hesitation.

"Have you been on any of the attractions?" he asked, then bit into his hot dog.

Sophie took a sip of her Coca-Cola.

"We went on the Ferris wheel. We were on our way to get some fairy floss."

Sophie cocked her head. "Fairy floss?"

"Spun sugar," Thaddeus clarified. "In a rainbow of colors."

Cotton candy, Sophie thought, but didn't say. "It sounds yummy."

"Ah, yes." Edith smiled and traded a quick glance with her husband. "It's very good. Yummy, as you might put it."

"You wanted to know how my meeting with the photographer went?" Ignoring his hot dog for the moment, Josiah focused on his sister and brother-in-law.

"Yes. I very much want to hear about the man from the *Gazette*." Thaddeus, a man as wide as he was tall, with thinning hair and a genial nature, leaned forward. "Did he bring his new camera?"

Edith glanced at Sophie.

"My husband is obsessed with still-life photography." Affection wove through Edith's words like a pretty ribbon. "He's very talented."

Thaddeus waved away the praise, though Sophie could see her words had pleased him. "I dabble."

Thaddeus's face remained bright with interest when he refocused on Josiah.

"He did bring the new Brownie with him," Josiah confirmed.

While both Edith and Thaddeus fixed their attention on

Josiah, Sophie picked up her hot dog and ate a couple of quick bites.

"He took a few test shots to test the lighting." Josiah slanted a glance in Sophie's direction. "He even took a couple of me with Sophie by the car."

Sophie, who'd just brought her bottle of Coke to her lips, froze when all eyes shifted to her.

"You were there?" Puzzlement filled Edith's gaze. "Why?"

"She came by to see me." Josiah spoke as if that was an everyday occurrence. "Our time together yesterday was cut short."

"You have spent time together two days in a row?" Edith blinked in surprise. "When were you introduced?"

Sophie opened her mouth to explain how they'd met, but closed it without speaking when she caught Josiah's barely perceptible headshake.

"Dear Sister, I wasn't aware I had to convey my social schedule to you." Josiah's voice, though smooth as silk, held a slight edge.

"You-you don't, of course," Edith backpedaled, lifting both hands, palms out. "I was merely curious as, er, ever since Daisy's passing—" She paused and cast a glance at Sophie.

"Sophie knows about Daisy. We've spoken of her."

Edith's eyes widened. "You don't speak of Daisy with anyone, not even family."

"Perhaps it is time," was all he said.

"Yes, well, perhaps it is," Edith agreed. "As I was saying, I'm curious how the two of you met."

"At the Chautauqua." Sophie smiled. "Your brother and I share a great love of learning."

"Were you there with your family?" Edith rushed out the question, obviously determined to gather as much information as possible before Josiah shut her down.

Sophie didn't blame her. She liked that Edith was bold enough to ask the questions on her mind. "I was—"

"I realize you have many questions, Sister, but Thaddeus also has questions about the camera and the photographer that I promised to answer." Josiah smiled easily. "Let me speak now about today's photography session."

While Josiah offered a blow-by-blow of the time in the showroom, Sophie listened and finished off her hot dog and Coke.

Edith appeared as interested in Josiah's account as her husband was.

"I am eager to see the photographs," Thaddeus said, "and to read the article in the newspaper. Do you know when they will run it?"

Josiah shook his head. "I don't, but as soon as they let me know, I'll tell you."

"Thaddaeus," Edith said, stepping into the brief silence. "I am dying for fairy floss. Perhaps you and Josiah could get some for Sophie and me while we remain here in the shade and become better acquainted."

Josiah glanced at Sophie, and she saw the question in his eyes. He wasn't asking only if she wanted cotton candy, but was she okay with him leaving her with his sister?

Sophie offered a reassuring smile. "I'd love some, too."

"If you're certain." Josiah rose, but made no move to leave, shifting from one foot to the other.

"Do go on, Josiah." Edith waved a dismissive hand. "Sophie will be safe with me."

"I really would like some fairy floss." Sophie's lighthearted tone appeared to allay Josiah's fears.

"We won't be away long." His eyes held a promise.

"Come on, Josiah." Thaddeus touched his shoulder, then gestured with his head. "Before the line gets too long."

"You won't wander off while we're gone, will you?" Josiah asked.

Edith rolled her eyes. "Where would we go? Besides, we want our treat."

Sophie wasn't certain why Josiah was so worried about leaving her with his sister, who appeared to be a perfectly nice woman. Then it struck her. Perhaps he feared she would disappear again the moment his back was turned. She wished she could explain that she'd had no idea when she stepped into that shed that it would take her away from him.

"I'll be right here when you return," Sophie assured Josiah.

The two men strolled off, Josiah casting one last glance over his shoulder before turning to speak with his brother-in-law.

"Sophie." Edith cleared her throat, drawing Sophie's attention back to the woman gazing at her with curious blue eyes.

"I'm sorry." Sophie gave a little laugh. "Woolgathering is a bad habit of mine."

"My brother likes you."

"I hope so." Sophie found herself glancing toward the spot where she'd last seen Josiah. "Because I'm rather fond of him."

"Yet, you only recently met."

"That is true." Sophie considered saying more, but decided to change the subject instead. "How did you and Thaddeus meet?"

"Thaddeus is an accountant. As is his father." Edith's lips curved. "They handle all the bookkeeping work for Huston Ford Baltimore and now GraceTown. Thaddeus stopped over to the house one day to drop off business papers, and my father made the introductions. When he asked if he could call on me, I said yes."

"The connection deepened, and you eventually married." Sophie fought a pang of envy at the thought of true love flowing so smoothly.

"Yes, after a year, Thaddeus went to my father and got his blessing and then proposed." Edith sighed. "I was over the moon with happiness to have found my true love. I was nearly five-and-twenty and still unmarried."

"That's not that old," Sophie began, then stopped, knowing that in this time, most women married by the age of twenty-one.

"You are, I believe, close to Josiah's age." Though Edith framed the words as a statement, Sophie heard the question.

"I am." Sophie glanced at her Coke bottle and wished it weren't empty, not because she was thirsty, but so she'd have something to do with her hands.

"Have you lost a spouse like Josiah has?" Edith inclined her head. "Someone you loved who is no longer with you? Is this grief something that you and my brother share?"

"I have never been married." Sophie kept her tone easy. "I have never been in love."

"You are a beautiful woman. I would think you'd have many beaus wanting to court you."

"I have not been as fortunate as you. There has been no one who captured my heart."

"My brother has captured your interest." Edith spoke in a matter-of-fact tone. "I'm sure you're aware he's a wealthy man."

"A man's wealth doesn't interest me." Sophie kept her gaze on Edith's face. "What a man is like inside is what interests me. Josiah is a kind, intelligent and interesting man. It is those qualities of his that attract me, nothing else."

Edith nodded. "He is a good man. I'm happy to see him here today, though I admit I was surprised. After Daisy's death—"

Edith paused and cast Sophie a speculative gaze.

"I know about Daisy and her death."

Edith's brow furrowed. "I will admit I'm surprised my brother spoke so openly to you about Daisy. He's very private, you see. At least he has been since losing her. He's been adamant that he no longer has any interest in courtship or marriage. I believe him." She hesitated and cleared her throat. "Or rather, I did."

"Everyone deals with grief differently and in their own time." Sophie shrugged. "How we feel at one moment isn't necessarily how we feel at another."

She was precluded from saying more by the return of Thaddeus and Josiah. The men's faces held broad smiles, and the swirling rainbow-colored spun sugar that Josiah handed her would have been enough for everyone at the table, except that Thaddeus had brought a similar one for Edith.

"Thank you, Josiah." Sophie smiled up at him. "I hope you will share this with me."

His answering smile arrowed straight to her heart.

Out of the corner of her eye, Sophie saw Thaddeus and Edith exchange a glance.

"Did you and my sister have a pleasant conversation?" Josiah asked.

"We did." Impulsively, Sophie reached over and squeezed Edith's hand. "Your sister is delightful."

"Sophie and I would have been content to sit here and converse all afternoon. But," Edith shifted her gaze and fluttered her dark lashes, "Thaddeus promised that we would go on the gondolas."

Thaddeus, who had remained standing, held out his hand and said, "I am a man of my word."

Giggling, Edith stood and grasped her husband's hand.

Immediately, Thaddeus's hand slipped around her waist. Then his gaze shifted to Josiah and Sophie. "It was a pleasure seeing you today. I hope to see you both again very soon."

"The pleasure was all mine." Sophie smiled at the couple.

"Will we see you again?" Edith asked her.

The innocent question struck at the heart of Sophie's fears.

Would she see Josiah again after today? She slipped her hand into her pocket and fingered the love token.

"If I have anything to say about it, you will," Josiah said, sounding almost jovial.

Sophie watched the couple stroll off, waving when Edith looked back for a second.

"My sister likes you." Josiah returned to his seat opposite Sophie.

"That makes me happy." Sophie offered him the cotton candy.

"I purchased it for you."

"I want to share."

Josiah took a wad of blue and put it into his mouth. His lips curved. "I'd forgotten how good fairy floss tastes."

When Sophie plucked some and popped it into her own mouth, Josiah eyes followed her actions.

"Your lips are pink and covered in sugar."

Using her tongue, Sophie swiped the sugar from her lips, a low ache forming in her abdomen at the sight of the hunger in Josiah's eyes. Not for the cotton candy. No, not for the sweet treat, but for her.

"Josiah," she began, leaning forward.

Instead of meeting her halfway, he sat back, and she was suddenly aware of their surroundings.

Later, she promised herself, there would be time for kisses. Lots and lots of kisses.

12

The moment Sophie saw the steeplechase horses, her lips curved into a wide smile. She shot an excited look at Josiah. "This is going to be fun."

They climbed a number of steps to an upper platform where they would mount a double-saddled wooden horse, then ride it down like a roller coaster.

When they reached the top, Josiah turned to her. "Do you know how it works?"

"Ah, not really."

"It's a gravity-driven ride. Our horse will compete with five others as we gain speed on the way down, then our momentum will carry us up the next hill. The race will go fast."

"I like fast." Her hazel eyes snapped with excitement. "I wish that I had on trousers. It would make the ride so much easier than messing with these skirts."

Josiah chuckled, then nodded. "You're probably right."

He stepped forward in line with her, his hand resting lightly against the small of her back.

The attendant, dressed like a jockey in a red silk shirt, white pants and matching cap, offered to assist Sophie onto their horse, but Josiah waved him away. Placing his hands on Sophie's waist, he lifted her up and onto the horse with ease.

"I hope you don't think me forward," he began, "but I think it best if we tuck your skirts more firmly around your legs so they don't get caught in any machinery."

Sophie smiled brightly. "Tuck away."

It felt strange, Josiah thought, folding the fabric and slipping it between her legs and the horse. Of course, there was no need for his fingers to wander any higher than her knee. Still, the intimacy of the gesture wasn't lost on him.

Once the task was completed, he swung himself up on the horse behind her, his arms slipping around her to take the reins.

Sophie looked over her shoulder at him. "I'm super excited."

If someone had told Josiah two days ago that he'd be at Funland on Friday, sitting behind a beautiful woman at the top of the steeplechase attraction, he'd have told them they were a crackpot.

Yet, here he was, and in this moment, there was nowhere else he'd rather be. "Sophie, I—"

A bugle sounded, and he had no time to say anything more.

"And you're off," the attendant shouted, releasing the mounts.

Sophie began to scream on the first drop.

Not out of fear, Josiah realized, but with pure joy.

Several pins that held her hair in place must have become dislodged, because soft strands the color of dark walnut brushed against his face.

His stomach might have pitched, and his heart certainly raced, but Josiah couldn't recall the last time he'd felt so alive.

Their horse came in third in the race, but that didn't matter to him or to Sophie.

When he swung her off the mount, she wobbled unsteadily,

so he put his arms around her until she steadied and stepped back from him.

"That was a blast."

He wasn't familiar with the term, but the excitement on her face had him agreeing.

"Let's do it again," she said.

"Your wish is my command." His mock bow brought her laughter bubbling out.

After the second time, they shifted their attention to the figure-eight roller coaster. When they finished their first ride, they planned to go again until they saw the long line.

They headed instead to the shorter line at the Ferris wheel.

"That was a—"

"Blast?" he suggested.

Something in the way he said the word made her smile. "Exactly."

The last of her pins were gone, and her hair tumbled wildly around her shoulders. Her cheeks were a bright pink, and her lips were rosy, though no trace of fairy floss remained.

"I love Ferris wheels." Sophie tipped her head back and glanced up into the sky.

For a moment, he was confused, until he remembered she'd been to Coney Island multiple times.

"When we're high in the sky," she told him, "it will be as if we're the only two people in the world."

Sophie's thigh pressed against his in the cart. With each cart holding eighteen people, there was no space for her to move over. But she didn't appear to mind the intimacy, and he liked the closeness.

In fact, as the cart jerked upward while the attendant filled the other carts, Josiah slipped an arm around her shoulders.

For a second, he worried he was being too bold, until Sophie looked at him and smiled. Then she rested her head against his shoulder. "This is turning out to be the most perfect day. Like one of those amazing dreams that you never want to wake up from."

He toyed with a lock of her hair, finding it even more soft and silky than it looked. "Thankfully, this isn't a dream. And we can come here again and enjoy it another time."

She expelled a breath. "I hope so."

"There is no reason we can't."

Sophie shifted her gaze, then pointed. "I want to go on that next."

Before she even finished speaking, Josiah was shaking his head. The parachute jump was too dangerous.

Josiah fought for an easy tone. "There's a chicken merry-go-round that was built in England. It's one of Funland's most popular attractions."

"We can do that after we go on that one." Her eyes lit up as the parachutes drifted down to the ground.

"Women don't go on that one."

Sophie narrowed her gaze. "I see a woman on it."

"Most women don't go on it." He tried, he really tried, to keep a note of finality from his voice, sensing she wouldn't respond well to any heavy-handedness.

Sophie only smiled, then kissed him on the cheek. "Haven't you figured out by now that I'm not most women?"

BY THE TIME she and Josiah had completed the parachute jump and then the chicken merry-go-round, Sophie was ready to enter the pavilion.

It was the ping-pong tables inside that drew Sophie's eye. She pointed. "Want to play?"

Surprise flickered in Josiah's blue depths. "You know how?"

"I do." She made a quick sweeping motion with one hand as if swatting a ball. "I'm very good at it, too, so play with me at your peril."

Josiah chuckled and shook his head. "I've never known anyone like you, Sophie Jessup."

"Well, I've never known anyone like you, so I would say we're even."

Despite her bravado, it had been a while since Sophie had played ping-pong. She'd learned the game from her dad, who'd been an avid player during his college years.

Her mom had little interest in the game and even less skill, so from the time Sophie had been small, it had been her and her dad facing off across the table in the basement.

Josiah won the first game. He was an adequate player, though he had a habit of hitting the ball too hard. Sophie remembered her father telling her to hit like Goldilocks—not too soft, not too hard, but just right.

Sophie knew Josiah's game would improve immensely if he spent just one evening with her father.

But her father would never meet Josiah. The two men would never have the chance to square off across a ping-pong table. Josiah wouldn't get to experience her father's corny jokes or discover what a wonderful woman her mother was.

Josiah sliced the corner, and Sophie blinked back tears as she bent to pick up the ball.

As if he sensed her distress, Josiah was at her side in an instant, reaching down to grab the ball before lightly grasping her arm.

He tipped up her chin with a curved finger, his gaze searching her face and appearing to take note of the tears glistening in her eyes.

"What is wrong, Sophie?"

The kindness and concern in his voice had a lump forming

in her throat. This man was simply the best. How was she going to live without him?

"I was just thinking how much my parents would like you."

"I'm sure that I will like them as well." Giving her arm a squeeze, he stepped back as if suddenly conscious of the speculative looks they were garnering.

Sophie drew in a deep breath. She would not ruin what was left of their day together.

"You may have caught me off-guard with that shot," she told him, "but this game is going to be mine."

Good humor replaced the worry in his eyes. "If you say so."

"I know so." She moved into position and picked up her paddle. "Show me what you've got. I'm ready."

Sophie leaned back against Josiah's arm as their gondola car sloshed its way through the pavilion's indoor river. Tables set up on either side in a decidedly Venetian theme reminded her of GraceTown's modern-day River Walk along Cripple Creek.

"This is the perfect way to end the day." She expelled a happy breath. "Sitting here with you is so relaxing."

"I've really enjoyed spending today with you, Sophie."

She glanced over and saw he was gazing at her intently. "What's the matter?"

He didn't deny that anything was amiss, as she expected. Instead, he gave a little laugh. "You'll think I'm foolish."

Sophie took his hand and met his gaze and trying to will him to see just how serious she was. "There isn't anything you can say to me that I will think foolish. If we can't talk with each other, share feelings with each other, what is the point?"

He nodded, but a sheepish look crossed his face. "I worry

that we'll get somewhere, and you'll disappear. Like you did yesterday. I turned around, and you were gone."

His expression grew serious. "I spent nearly an hour searching for you. I looked everywhere. It was as if you'd vanished. I had no way to locate you because I didn't know where you live or work."

"I'm sorry about that," Sophie began, but he lifted a hand.

"I worry that's going to happen again. That we'll have a wonderful day, like the one we've enjoyed together this day, then you'll vanish." His gaze searched hers. "This time, you came back. Perhaps you won't next time."

Sophie wished she could assure Josiah his fears were baseless, but how could she? All she knew right now was the third tent hadn't been there until she'd put the love token in her pocket. Only then had she been able to see the tent and step into 1916.

Before she attempted to explain the unexplainable, she needed to have as much information as possible.

"Sophie." Josiah rested a hand on her arm. "I realize we've only known each other a very short time, but I think, I believe, that I'm falling in love with you. I don't want to lose you."

13

During nice weather, the River Walk along Cripple Creek drew visitors and locals alike to the shops, bars and bistros on both sides of the water.

Sophie wasn't sure if it was the weather, the Chautauqua being in town or simply that it was a Friday night that had her energy flagging as she wove her way through the hordes of people on her way to meet Ruby.

She hoped her time with her friend would be a recharge.

After making plans with Josiah to meet at the fairgrounds tomorrow, she'd had him drive her to a spot just outside the entrance to the fairgrounds. He had wanted to see her home, but Sophie had been able to convince him she had a personal errand to run at the fair. Being a gentleman, he'd eventually, if reluctantly, agreed to say good-bye and drop her off rather than accompany her inside. Once he'd gone, she'd made her way to the shed where she'd seen the puppy the day before, stepped inside and had been immediately transported back to the present. No head rush or shakiness this time.

Sophie's lips quirked upward. It appeared she'd become a

natural at time travel. She wasn't going to obsess over the logistics, content to accept for now that they were what they were.

She spotted the sign for Red Top Bistro and Wine Bar and picked up her pace. Seconds later, Sophie smiled. Her friend had scored a primo table near the water's edge.

A brunette with cat-eye glasses looked up when Sophie approached the hostess stand.

Sophie gestured to the completely full outdoor seating area. "My friend is already here."

Ruby set her phone aside when Sophie approached.

"You did good, Ruby. I love this table." Sophie dropped into the metal chair that managed to be both comfortable and stylish.

"I got here at the right time." Ruby smiled. "I had the server leave menus. I wasn't sure if we were eating or just drinking."

Sophie thought of the hot dog and fairy floss she'd consumed with Josiah a century ago. She couldn't stop the chuckle.

"I know that smile." Ruby's eyes snapped with excitement. "You're going to tell me everything."

"I will." Sophie picked up the menu. "Let's order first."

Since she'd eaten mostly junk today, Sophie perused the salad offerings, then closed the menu.

Ruby took a sip of wine. "That was quick."

"Their honey blue salad is my favorite."

Ruby considered. "I'll have that, too."

"What are you drinking?"

"Riesling."

"That should go well with the blue cheese in the salad." The way her mind was racing, Sophie was glad not to have to make too many decisions.

A server appeared and took their order, returning moments later with Sophie's glass of wine.

Sophie took a sip and felt herself relax. "I'm so glad it worked for us to get together this evening."

"I expected you'd be tired after two days of volunteering in the heat, but you look..." Ruby continued to study her with an intensity that had Sophie shifting uncomfortably. "Different. Happier than I've seen you in a while."

"Happier?" Even as she said the word, Sophie couldn't help but smile. "What do you mean by that?"

Ruby tapped a finger against her bright-red lips. "I'm not exactly sure. How was yesterday? And today? Was volunteering what you expected?"

Sophie chuckled and shook her head. "Not at all what I expected." She took another sip of her Riesling and told herself she wasn't stalling. She simply wasn't certain where to begin.

"I'll start at the beginning," she murmured.

"Always a good place."

"My job was to make sure the performers in each of the *two* tents had everything they needed." Sophie released her glass and began to fiddle with her napkin.

"Was Dylan supposed to handle one of the tents?"

"Actually, he was supposed to do cleanup between the speakers."

"No wonder he bailed." Ruby rolled her eyes. "The guy has never been much for manual labor."

Sophie's hand stilled. "That's not true."

"Sure it is. Remember when we got back from Baltimore after buying all that stuff at the Wexman estate sale? Dylan stopped by just as it was time for us to unload the van." Ruby laughed. "I swear he was making up excuses for why he suddenly had to turn around and leave before we opened the back doors."

Sophie thought back to that day. "I guess I didn't make the connection."

"You've always cut him a lot of slack."

"Well, maybe I'm ready to stop that."

"I hope so. You deserve better." Ruby lifted her wineglass in a salute to her friend, then took a healthy sip.

Sophie's thoughts immediately turned to Josiah. She couldn't imagine him hurrying off when there was work to be done.

As Ruby lowered her glass, her eyes remained on Sophie. "I still don't understand your emphasis on the two tents."

"Okay." Sophie held up both hands. "Fair warning. This is going to sound a little crazy."

She laid it all out for Ruby, not skimping on any details.

"Do you really think you stepped through some kind of time warp?" Ruby's gaze turned assessing when, instead of immediately replying, Sophie paused to take a drink of wine.

"At first, I thought I was dreaming, and that's how I presented it to my mom, as a really vivid dream. But the thing is, Ruby, it wasn't a dream." Sophie reached into her tiny bag and pulled out the love token. She set the coin on the table. "This was in my pocket. I know it sounds unbelievable, but I believe having this with me gives me access to the third tent like it's some kind of portal."

Ruby picked up the coin, turning it over and over in her fingers the way she had yesterday morning. Then she handed the love token back to Sophie. "I suppose anything is possible."

"Josiah is wonderful, Ruby. The connection we share is so powerful. I've never felt this way about anyone before." Sophie suddenly found herself having to blink back tears. "When he kisses me... Heck, just when I'm with him, it's as if I'm right where I'm meant to be, and all is right in my world."

Ruby scanned Sophie's face, but said nothing.

"He lives in the past. My life is here," Sophie said. "The thought of being without him makes me incredibly sad."

"You're lucky, you know."

"How do you figure?"

"You've experienced the kind of love we all dream of finding." An emotion Sophie couldn't identify swept across Ruby's face. "Even if it's short-lived, you've had something some of us will never find."

"I won't let what is building between us go." Sophie straightened in her seat. "I'm determined to find a way for us to be together."

"I wish I could meet him."

"I wish you could, too." Sophie tapped her fingers against the table. "I wonder if I can take someone with me. We could go to the fairgrounds and give it a try."

"Do we have to be at the fairgrounds, or could we do it from here?"

As the server set down their salads, Sophie smiled at the thought of them poofing to 1916 from where they sat. "I don't believe it'll work from just anywhere."

"How do you know?" Ruby stabbed some greens and a grape with her fork. "Have you tried?"

"I had the love token in my purse when I went to the fairgrounds this morning, and nothing happened until I put it in my pocket." Sophie took a bite of salad and chewed thoughtfully. "I've determined it has to be in my pocket, not in a purse or in my hand, for the tent to appear."

"And the tent only appears when you're at the fairgrounds?"

"Yes, somehow all this seems tied to the Chautauqua." Sophie inhaled sharply as a realization struck. "You know what this means?"

Ruby shook her head.

"Once the Chautauqua ends on Monday, my portal, or whatever you want to call the tent, will be gone." Sophie's heart sank. "I won't be able to get back to Josiah."

"You don't know that." Ruby's matter-of-fact tone tempered Sophie's rising panic. "You need more information. That's why we need to go to the fairgrounds and do some experimenting."

AFTER FINISHING THEIR MEAL, Sophie agreed to meet Ruby by the tents at the fairgrounds. As she was leaving the bistro, she paused and changed course when some friends of her parents called out her name and motioned her over to their table.

Thankfully, the foursome's food came a moment later, so the conversation was brief. Sophie couldn't wait to get to the fairgrounds.

She was nearly to her car when she saw Dylan, blond hair glistening in the glow of the streetlights, leaning against a car. It wasn't his car, unless he'd bought it since she'd last seen him. More than likely, it belonged to the pretty brunette who had her arms looped around his neck while his hands rested on her waist.

Sophie watched as Dylan pulled the brunette up against him and brought his lips to hers. She watched the woman run her fingers through his hair. She watched Dylan's hand slide into the back pocket of her shorts and listened as the woman giggled through their kiss.

Maybe she should feel hurt or angry. Or...something. And yet, despite the fact that Dylan was technically her boyfriend, the only thought that came to Sophie's mind was, *Will I kiss Josiah again?*

The fact was, she didn't care who Dylan kissed, because he didn't matter to her. If she was being honest, he hadn't mattered to her for a while now.

When the young woman—who couldn't have been more

than twenty—slid behind the wheel of her red convertible, Dylan leaned over and kissed her again.

"See you tomorrow at the lake," the brunette called as she backed out of the space and zoomed off down the street.

Sophie hadn't planned on seeing Dylan today, but it appeared this was one of those meant-to-be moments.

A smile lingered on Dylan's lips as he watched the car until it disappeared from sight. Then he turned and saw Sophie. The smile slipped away for a whole five seconds before making its return. "Sophie, I didn't see you there."

"You were too busy kissing your girlfriend." Sophie strolled past him to her car, which was parked close to where the brunette's had been.

"Sophie, that was...I mean, she's no one."

"Looked like she was someone. Will she be at the lake with you tomorrow?" Sophie wasn't sure why she asked.

"Will you still be volunteering?"

"You know I will. I committed to the entire festival."

Dylan made a face. "See, that's the problem. You gave up a whole weekend without even thinking about me."

"I did think about you. You said you would volunteer with me. We were supposed to be there together."

"Why would I want to spend my weekend volunteering? I want to do *fun* things with you, Sophie. Between your shop and your family and stuff like this, you don't make time for *fun*."

It appeared turning the tables on her was how he intended to handle this. Sophie found she didn't much care.

"You're right. You and I are too different." The rightness of her decision had the words coming easily. "I don't think we should see each other again."

Stepping off the curb, she opened her car door. Before she could slip inside, she felt his hand on her arm.

Exhaling a breath, she turned. "What is it?"

His brows were pulled together in confusion. "Just like that?"

"Just like what?" She thought what she'd said was clear and actually something he wanted, too. They hadn't been right for each other from the beginning. But he'd been charming, and she hadn't looked too deep.

"Just like that, we're done?" He studied her face for a long moment. "I thought we meant something to each other."

Sophie wanted to laugh at his audacity. She'd literally just seen him kissing another woman. Then her expression softened. She didn't kid herself that Dylan cared deeply for her. Odds were he simply wanted to be the one to call it off. Still, she reminded herself, they'd had some good times.

She offered a conciliatory smile. "Dylan, there's no reason to make this hard. You and I, we're too different for there to be more than friendship between us."

"But—"

"I hope you find what you're looking for." Sophie knew he still struggled with not only personal relationships, but figuring out his place in the world. "No hard feelings."

He searched her face. "I really did like you, you know."

"I know. I'll see you around." Sliding behind the wheel, Sophie left the window up, not wanting a good-bye kiss from him.

"Someone is having a good time." Ruby smiled as raucous laughter came from one of the tents on the fairgrounds.

A booming voice could be heard from the second tent.

"These should be the last performances of the day," Sophie told her friend. "I told Alcidean I'd be happy to stay and work some evening shifts, too, but she'd already scheduled volunteers to staff the later hours."

"Which is good, because it gives us time to experiment." Ruby's gaze sharpened. "Where's the coin?"

"It's in my purse." Sophie took out the love token and slid it into the front pocket of her jeans, then shifted her gaze to look for the third tent. She smiled and turned to Ruby. "Do you see it?"

"See what?"

Sophie gestured. "The tent is right there."

Ruby shook her head. "I don't see anything."

Though disappointment surged, Sophie told herself this was what she'd expected. Alcidean had said she hadn't seen the tent, and she was at the fairgrounds all the time.

"Put the coin in your pocket," Sophie instructed. But when Ruby reached for it, she didn't immediately release it. "If you step into the tent, the only exits are to 1916. If that happens, there's a white shed nearby. Entering that will bring you right back."

Once Sophie released the coin, Ruby put it in her pocket.

Ruby's gaze scanned the surroundings. She shook her head and handed the love token back to Sophie. "No third tent."

Sophie slipped the coin back into her own pocket and held out her hand. "Take my hand."

Ruby took it.

"Do you see it now?"

"I don't."

"Okay." Sophie kept hold of Ruby's hand. "Let's walk into the tent together and—"

But when Sophie tried to step inside with Ruby, the tent disappeared. She expelled a sigh. "Doesn't work."

"Darn. I was really looking forward to spending my evening in 1916." Ruby flashed a smile, then her expression turned serious. "Could Josiah come back with you?"

"I'm not sure how that would work. If it won't let you into the tent—"

"But you said you come back via a shed," Ruby reminded her. "Does he see the shed?"

Sophie's brow furrowed as she tried to remember. This morning when she'd gone back to 1916, he hadn't been at the fair at all. And yesterday, he hadn't seen her go into the shed, though she couldn't say for sure if he'd ever seen it. She shook her head. "I'm not totally sure about the shed. But even if he could come back with me, would he be able to get back to 1916? Or would he be stuck here forever?"

"The way you'd be stuck there once the Chautauqua ends?"

Sophie nodded. "I'm actually more worried about not being able to get back to Josiah once the Chautauqua ends than staying there forever."

Surprise skittered across Ruby's face. "Wait. Are you saying you're seriously considering staying there?"

"I am." Sophie smiled at Ruby's sudden look of horror. "Considering it, that is."

Ruby took Sophie's arm and began to walk with her at a fast clip.

"Where are we going?"

"My mind is buzzing. I need to think."

They'd gone only a few feet when Ruby released her hold on Sophie's arm and came to an abrupt stop. "Have you thought about what it would be like to live in that time?"

Sophie cocked her head. "You're referring to the lack of technology?"

"I'm referring to the lack of modern medicine, to the World War that will soon be upon them, to the friggin' Spanish flu in 1918 that killed one in five people who caught it." Distress had Ruby's voice pitching high. "You could go back there only to have Josiah die. Or you could die. Maybe from some simple infection that's no big deal today. Do you hear what I'm saying?"

Before Sophie could respond, Ruby blew out a breath and turned. She took three steps, then whirled back. "I don't mean to lecture. God knows I hate it when someone does that to me. I just want you to really think about your decision. All that to say, I also want you to be happy."

Her friend looked so miserable that Sophie wrapped her arms around her and hugged her tight before stepping back.

"I get it, Ruby. I hear what you're saying, and you have my word that I won't make any hasty decisions." Sophie met Ruby's gaze. "I'll be giving this a lot of thought."

14

The next morning when Sophie stepped from the tent, Josiah greeted her with a hug.

The smile that lifted his lips when he spotted her had her resolve faltering. Though she knew she needed to tell him what was going on, she wasn't sure how to start.

"What shall we do today?" He looked particularly handsome in his cream-colored linen suit.

"Let's go for a drive." She kept her tone light. "Maybe back to Culler Lake."

The trip was a short one. She instructed him to pull the car beneath the leafy branches of a large oak tree.

Sophie wiped suddenly sweaty palms against the soft fabric of her pale pink dress. Now that the Tin Lizzie had stopped, and she and Josiah were alone, truly alone, she could delay no longer.

Would she be foolish to confide in him? She would be asking a lot of him, she knew. It was difficult enough for her to accept that she'd traveled back in time. How could she expect him to believe it?

"Sophie." Turning in his seat, Josiah reached over and took her hand. Worry creased his brow. "Is something wrong?"

It seemed fitting they were at Culler Lake, where she'd begun falling in love with him that first day.

She squeezed his hand. "There's something I need to tell you."

"What is it?" He searched her face.

Sophie licked her suddenly dry lips, and she realized her throat had gone bone-dry. "Ah, you don't happen to have a throat lozenge or something on you?"

"I have something you might like." He pulled a tiny circle of peppermints wrapped in tinfoil out of his pocket. "They're called Pep-O-Mint Life Savers. They're supposed to be breath mints, but one should work as a throat lozenge."

Taking one of the mints, Sophie offered Josiah a smile and popped it into her mouth.

"Better?" Josiah asked after a few moments of silence.

"Yes, thank you." Sophie quickly considered whether it would be best to tell Josiah about the love token while sitting in the car, or would being out in the sunshine have words coming to her more easily?

Then again, what she was going to tell him would have the power to knock him off his feet. Best to remain in the car, she decided.

"It's a beautiful day, isn't it?"

"It is," he agreed, "but we didn't drive all the way here to discuss the weather."

If his tone had been anything but filled with gentle kindness, she might have reconsidered what she was about to say. But this was Josiah, and he deserved more. He deserved better. He deserved the truth.

Where should she start? With her business? With attending

the Wexman estate auction in Baltimore and bidding on the trunk and boxes?

She decided to start small and go from there. "Several days ago, this came into my possession."

Reaching into her pocket, Sophie pulled out the love token and handed it to Josiah. "Do you know what it is?"

He turned it over in his fingers. Unlike Ruby, he didn't appear surprised by the etchings on the one side.

"It's a love token." He inclined his head. "When you say it came into your possession, are you telling me a gentleman caller gave it to you?"

"No. No. Nothing like that." Sophie couldn't believe his mind would go there. Then she realized almost immediately that it made sense that it had. Love tokens had still been a "thing" in 1916. "I was going through the contents of an old steamer chest I'd purchased and found it."

Josiah handed it back to her, his eyes never leaving her face. "What does that have to do with us?"

"I know that you're a practical man, but I also believe you have an open mind." Sophie kept her voice even. "For what I'm about to tell you, that mind needs to be kept wide open."

His gaze turned watchful.

"I believe this token has the ability to transport me through time."

A look of surprise had his eyes widening. "That's—"

"Before you say that's crazy or unbelievable or simply can't be, let me explain." Sophie took a deep breath, then plunged ahead. "I live in the twenty-first century. I own an antique store in modern-day GraceTown. That's how I came across this coin. I bid on a trunk at an estate auction, and one of the items inside was this love token."

Josiah fixed his gaze on Sophie's face. His expression

remained inscrutable. Just when Sophie thought she couldn't bear his silence a moment more, he said, "Tell me everything."

Clasping her hands in her lap, Sophie took a deep breath and began.

"GraceTown—my GraceTown, I mean—is holding an end-of-summer Chautauqua. As a business owner, I'm active in the community. I volunteered to help. I've been in charge of making sure the performers have what they need in the two tents the city erected on the fairgrounds. But during my first shift as a volunteer, I saw there were actually three tents instead of two. I stepped into the third and noticed that everyone was dressed in 1916 fashion."

"Why was that such a surprise?"

"Because that's not how people dress in the twenty-first century." She managed a little smile. "Though everyone was encouraged to dress in period garb, not all, or really not even the majority, did. As a volunteer, I did, of course." Sophie paused, waiting for him to say... She wasn't sure what.

He only gazed expectantly at her.

Taking a deep breath, she continued. "When I stepped outside the tent, I realized I was no longer in my present time. I was here." She gestured with one hand. "In 1916. I could tell because of the horses and buggies and old-fashioned cars. Before that day, I'd only seen a Model T in a car museum."

"What kind of cars do you drive?"

With his love of motorized vehicles, it figured he'd go there first. "Cars with air conditioning and heated seats. Cars that can drive themselves and will automatically apply the brakes when sensors alert them to a potential accident. Some engines still run on gasoline. Others, called hybrids, run either on gas or electric. Lately, there are more vehicles that run only on electricity."

"That's fascinating." Josiah's eyes lit up, though his brow remained creased. "Unbelievable, but fascinating."

"When I found myself in this, well, this different world, it scared me. I didn't know what was happening. Was I dreaming? Had I fallen and hit my head? Was I hallucinating? Then you spoke with me."

"You were white as a ghost," he said, and she could see he was looking back.

"You were kind to me." Her eyes filled with tears. "You were so very kind to me."

When Josiah reached out a hand, Sophie took it as a drowning sailor might grasp a life preserver.

"When you left me... When you leave me to go back to the future..." He spoke in a rusty tone, as if his voice hadn't been used for a long time. "How do you get there?"

"The first time, there was this dog, a puppy. He was frightened. When you stopped to speak with a customer, I went to pick him up." Though her breath wanted to come in short puffs, Sophie forced herself to breathe slowly. "He darted into a small storage shed. When I stepped inside, I was back in my time."

"Had you been missed? You'd spent the day with me."

Sophie took the question as a positive. Perhaps she was being naïve, but he had to at least be considering what she'd said might be true to ask for clarification.

"It was as if I'd never left," she told him. "As if only a minute, or even a second, had passed."

"You mentioned that you spoke with your parents that night about me."

"I didn't know what had happened to me. I was still confused. I went to dinner with them that evening and told them I'd had this dream where I'd met this wonderful guy."

"In your dream."

She nodded. "My mother analyzes dreams. She thought it was my subconscious telling me that Dylan isn't the right man for me. That I deserve someone better." Sophie blew out a breath. "The thing was, it didn't feel like a dream. But the only other possibility was I was hallucinating, and that didn't feel right either. Being with you felt so real. And I was desperate to see you again."

Josiah rubbed his chin. After what felt like an eternity, he asked, "How did you get back here again?"

"At first, I thought the third tent was the key. I asked the volunteer coordinator about a third tent, but she said there was no third tent."

"She doesn't see the tent you see."

"No one can." Sophie shook her head. "So then I thought that this love token must be involved. I took my friend Ruby with me to the fairgrounds last night. She can't see the tent either, not even with the love token in her own pocket. I can't see it without the coin being in my pocket. Then, when I tried to lead her in—"

"You tried bringing her with you?"

Sophie nodded. "I held her hand and tried to step into the tent with her. But it disappeared then." She lifted a hand. "Before you ask me how and why it works only for me, I don't know. All I know is the love token has to be in my pocket. And I have to be able to see the third tent at the fairgrounds." Her lips quirked upward. "I even tried saying, 'Take me back to Josiah,' while the coin was in my hand. It didn't work."

His gaze grew thoughtful. "Do you still think this could be a dream?"

"No." Her little laugh pitched high. "I don't know how it happened, but this," she gestured with her hand between them, "is real. I know it is real. You are real. What I feel for you is real."

He said nothing for the longest time.

"I'll prove it," she said, desperation causing her to speak quickly. "We'll return to the fairgrounds, and you can watch me go back."

"Sophie," he began, then stopped as if unsure what he wanted to say.

She heaved a heavy sigh. "I understand it sounds crazy."

"I believe you." His voice was strong and his gaze direct. "It makes no sense, but I believe in you, in what I feel for you, in how powerfully we are connected."

With the emotion rising inside her, clogging her throat, the best Sophie could manage was a nod.

"Whatever this miracle is—and that's how I see this—I'm grateful."

Her heart swelled. She felt the same.

"What about Dylan?"

Sophie blinked.

"What part does he play in your life?"

"He plays no part. Not anymore." Sophie thought about telling Josiah about seeing Dylan with the brunette, but realized that story might be a bit too scandalous for 1916 sensibilities. "I ran into Dylan last night. I realized whatever was between us is truly gone and over. I told him I don't want to see him anymore."

Was that relief she saw in Josiah's eyes?

"How did he take the news?"

"Well, I don't think he liked being dumped, but it's only his pride that's wounded, not his heart."

JOSIAH WASN'T familiar with the term *dumped*, but he assumed it meant the man was out of her life. That, he realized, made him happy.

"The way I see it," Sophie continued, "is some people come into your life for a season, while others are there for a lifetime."

"You're saying Dylan was there for a season, and that's okay?"

"Yes." Her gaze turned contemplative. "I believe when you're in a relationship, you learn a lot about yourself. Everyone we meet or interact with has the potential to effect change in us."

"And you think being in a relationship with Dylan changed you."

"I do. I discovered what I want and don't want in a person I'm spending time with. I also learned the importance of letting go, of not hanging on to something that isn't working." Sophie flashed a quick smile. "If I hadn't let go of him, I wouldn't be fully open to considering a relationship with someone else. Someone like you."

Josiah smiled. "What you've said makes a good amount of sense."

"I think so." Sophie inclined her head. "What do you think you learned from your relationship with Daisy?"

The unexpected question had the smile slipping from his lips, and when he spoke, his voice held an edge. "Daisy was my wife."

"Marriage is a relationship," Sophie pointed out.

If she'd noticed his terse tone, she gave no indication. "Daisy and I got along splendidly."

A softness filled Sophie's eyes. "A true love match."

"It was. Daisy taught me to be a better communicator about what I was feeling and thinking." Josiah's lips lifted. How many times had his wife told him that she couldn't read his mind? "Although we saw eye to eye on most things, when we didn't, I learned to say what I was feeling, to let her know what I needed."

"She sounds like an amazing woman." Sophie's voice was now as soft as her eyes.

"She was." Josiah cleared his throat. "I was convinced I'd never find anyone like her again."

"I can see that," Sophie agreed.

"Now I've come to realize that I've found someone who is

just as amazing." His lips quirked upward. "Even if she is from the future."

"I DON'T WANT you to go back." As he drove back to the fairgrounds, Josiah fought the fear creeping up his spine like a spider.

"I have to go back. People will miss me." She gave him a reassuring smile. "I'll come back here tomorrow."

His mind had been whirling as they rode back to the fairgrounds. For most of the drive, Sophie had remained silent, the love token clutched between her fingers.

Josiah had read novels about time travel, but those were fiction, and most involved machines. If Sophie was correct, it was the coin in her hand that held the power to transport her more than a hundred years back in time.

In a way, it explained a great deal—her odd turn of phrase and her bold behavior. Sophie was like no one else he knew because she was from a different world.

"How do you know when you step out of the tent that you'll come back to this time?" he asked, wondering why the thought hadn't occurred to him before now. "How do you know that you won't end up in 1860? Or 1752?"

She turned, and her hazel eyes clouded. "I don't know. After the first time brought me here, I assumed I'd end up here the next time, but you're right. I don't know for certain."

"Likewise, when you step into the shed, how do you know you'll end up back in your own time?" Josiah wondered how speaking of something so farfetched could seem so completely normal.

Even as he spoke the words and her face blanched, worry for her spiked.

"I-I never considered I could be, well, transported somewhere else."

"You should stay here," he told her. "It isn't safe. You could end up somewhere dangerous. Somewhere where you would be all alone."

"I don't think so." Though she tried to sound confident, he could see she was nowhere near as confident as she wanted him to believe. "Besides, I have to go back. My parents will be frantic with worry if I suddenly disappear. I can't do that to them."

"I will be frantic with worry, too." He spoke in a measured tone. "I'll worry that you've ended up in a time other than your own."

"I think we're okay for the next two days while the Chautauqua is going on." She hesitated. "After that, there will be decisions to make."

"You'll come back tomorrow?"

"I will."

"Same time?"

She nodded.

"I'll be here waiting." Josiah wheeled the car into the parking area, his fingers tightening on the steering wheel. "What if you go into that shed, and nothing happens?"

"Well, then," she blew out a breath, "I guess 1916 would be my new home."

He hopped out of the car and rounded the front to reach her just as she stepped out. His gaze searched the hazel depths of her eyes. "Would that make you sad?"

"Being in a time period where you are?" Rising on tiptoes, she brushed her lips with his. "Never."

~

Sophie placed the love token in the pocket of her dress as they approached the shed. She hadn't fully considered where she might end up when she stepped into the tent or the shed.

She hadn't considered she might end up in another time period altogether or somewhere dangerous. There also had been no worries about not being able to see Josiah again, because she hadn't been fully convinced that he was real.

Knowing he was real changed everything.

He took her hand, grasping it tightly in his, and she felt herself steady. When they reached the shed, he put his hands on her shoulders and gently turned her to face him. "You don't have to go. You can stay here. I will—"

"I need to go back," she told him. "I need to prepare my parents for the possibility of my staying in this time."

"They won't want—"

"You don't know them." She found herself wishing both her parents could have the chance to meet this wonderful man. Her mother would like his bright, inquisitive mind. Her dad would like his adventurous spirit and the way he treated her with such respect. "They want me to be happy. They said they would understand if I met someone and wanted to move away."

His lips curved ever so slightly. "I feel certain they weren't thinking of you moving to another century."

The laugh that bubbled up in her throat eased some of the tension that held her chest in a stranglehold. "I'm sure not."

"You'll come back to me tomorrow," he said, gazing into her eyes.

"I will." She took a breath and blew it out. She thought about adding *unless something unforeseen happens*, but didn't want to worry him any more than necessary. "I'll come at the same time."

"I'll be here waiting," he assured her, his gaze strong and direct.

"You run a business," she reminded him.

"Tomorrow is Sunday. All the businesses in town are closed on the Sabbath."

Sophie couldn't recall a time when that had been the norm, but she knew her parents would. "Good."

"It wouldn't matter what day it is." His eyes met hers. "There's only one place I want to be, and that's with you."

Glancing at the partially open door of the shed, Sophie squared her shoulders. Whirling back to him, she grabbed Josiah by his suit lapels and gave him a ferocious kiss.

Without giving herself a chance to chicken out, she rushed into the shed.

A second later, she found herself blinking in the bright midday sunshine.

Out of the corner of her eye, she saw Alcidean hurrying toward her. For a second, she thought she'd been missed.

"Alcidean, I didn't expect to see you out and about."

"I do like to venture out of the administration building every now and then." The woman shot her a warm smile. "I've heard such good things about Coates and Gilbert that I thought I'd catch part of their show."

"They're really good," Sophie said automatically.

"Then I'm glad I came to see them." Alcidean smiled. "By the way, I have more than enough volunteers for tomorrow, so if you have other plans, you don't need to come."

"Thank you. I do have some matters to attend to, but I may stop by in the morning to catch a couple of the acts."

"Perfectly fine." Alcidean let her gaze shift around the fairgrounds. "There's something about the 1910s. It was such a simpler, sweeter time."

"Yes." Sophie thought about Josiah, and her lips curved. "That time definitely has a lot to recommend it."

15

Once Sophie turned on the phone she'd left in her car, the repeated dings told her it wasn't only her parents who'd have missed her if she hadn't returned from 1916.

LMK if you still have dolphin wind chime by EOD. Mom's BD is Monday. D

The text from Dylan had Sophie shaking her head. She hadn't expected him to hold a grudge over the breakup, but she also hadn't expected him to text the next day about a gift for his mother.

The vintage wind chime with a dolphin at the top and a bell of copper bronze patina with seven bars hanging below had been in her shop for several months. She considered it a steal at fifty dollars, but it had been slow to move.

It's $50. LMK if you want me to set it back for you.

The answer came quickly.

Sold! PTPU Monday. Thx D

It didn't surprise her that Dylan would wait until Monday to pick it up. He'd likely be at the lake with his new girlfriend all weekend. A fact that didn't bother her at all.

She liked his comment and made a mental note to set the wind chime under the counter.

She dealt with another five texts—three about an upcoming meeting of the Economic Development Commission, one from her mother asking if she could fill in Tuesday night for one of her bridge partners who was going to be out of town, and the last was from Ruby reminding her about the house party tonight at Hannah and Charlie's.

Sophie expelled the breath she hadn't realized she'd been holding. Obviously, Ruby wasn't upset with her about last night.

She added a heart to Ruby's message, then texted, *I'll be there!*

Turning her attention to her emails, Sophie slogged her way through them, some business-related, some personal, before finally driving to Timeless Treasures.

As it was Saturday and still tourist season, both Andrew and Ruby were on the schedule for today. Which was good, Sophie thought, as she stepped through the front door and saw the number of people in her store.

Andrew was helping a gentleman with snow-white hair who appeared interested in several vintage picture frames. Ruby was ringing up a man who had a counter full of small purchases, while two others waited patiently in line behind him.

"How's it going?" she asked Ruby.

"Wonderful." Ruby flashed a broad smile. "We've been busy since we opened the doors this morning."

Out of the corner of her eye, Sophie caught sight of the dolphin wind chime. Stepping over, she carefully lifted it from where it hung over a sea glass exhibit and placed it under the counter, then affixed a sticky note with Dylan's name.

At Ruby's curious glance, Sophie smiled. "Dylan will be by on Monday to buy it."

"Sounds good." Ruby turned her attention to the next customer. "These cereal boxes have been so popular."

"My sister is a big *Star Wars* fan." The young woman, her hair in soft butterfly locs, smiled at the box. "She's going to love this *Star Wars* Obi-Wan Kenobi box."

"I'm sure she will." Ruby smiled brightly at the woman, then turned to Sophie. "Last month's bills are on your desk."

"Thanks." Sophie answered several questions from customers on her way to the back stairs, including one about her dress.

By the time she climbed the steps and reached her apartment, Sophie felt as if she'd put in a full day.

Some of it had to do with all the day-to-day demands. Some because of her conversation with Josiah. She had to admit she'd been a little freaked when she'd stepped into the shed.

Though she wanted nothing more than to stretch out on her bed for a few minutes, she needed to change and head over to her parents' house for an early dinner. From there, she would drive to Charlie and Hannah's house.

Had her life always been so hectic? Or did it simply feel that way because she'd experienced the calm of 1916?

She slipped off her hat and carefully set it aside before removing her dress.

Then she remembered the love token. Slipping it out of the pocket, she placed it on her nightstand. She stared at it for a long moment, recalling everything that had happened since she'd first discovered it in the steamer trunk.

She couldn't deny her growing love for Josiah. But could she really give up her modern-day life for love? Could she leave her parents and friends behind and never see them again? All for a man who—however powerful the connection between them felt—she'd only recently met?

On the other hand, the thought of going through life without him was unimaginable.

The turbulent thoughts and emotions had her head spinning.

Dropping down on the bed, she was tempted to simply crawl under the covers, pull them up over her head and block out the world.

She didn't have time. Dressing quickly, she slapped on some lip gloss and ran a brush through her hair. After glancing at the mirror, she decided she was ready.

In a matter of minutes, Sophie stood on the sidewalk in front of her childhood home, gazing at the two-story Cape Cod. Lights shone through the windows like welcoming beacons.

The scents of flowers from the bushes and various planters on the porch teased her nostrils. She'd grown up in this home, with the people inside. Could she really go the rest of her life never seeing them again?

Perhaps coming here had been a mistake.

After all, was she really going to tell her parents what she was considering?

Then again, how could she not? It wouldn't be fair to them for her to simply disappear without a trace.

As she was contemplating her options, the front door opened, and Bentley, the cockapoo her parents treated like a second child, stepped out onto the porch with her father.

For a second, neither the dog nor the man spotted her. Then Bentley let out a couple of low woofs and scrambled down the steps.

"Bentley," her father called out. "Stay."

Bentley was already racing across the yard to greet her. The wriggling mass of red fur and lapping tongue had her laughing as she crouched down to give him the rubs he expected.

"I'm happy to see you, too, boy." She shook her head as he flopped to his back, looking for a belly rub.

"Sophie." Her dad strode down the walkway toward her, a smile of pleasure on his lips. "I didn't realize you were here. I didn't hear the car drive up."

"You know the motors in these new cars. Super quiet." Sophie thought of the *chug-chug* of the Model T.

"Bentley." Her father pointed to the grass. "Go potty."

The dog cast a glance at Sophie.

"Go ahead," she urged. "I'm not going anywhere."

Apparently satisfied, Bentley strode to a bush and lifted his leg.

"We're glad you could come to dinner." Her dad gave her a quick hug. "Especially since you mentioned going to some party tonight."

"Just a casual house party." Sophie waved a dismissive hand. "It should be fun."

"If you're going there after leaving here, sounds like a late night." He chuckled as if realizing what he'd just said. He shook his head. "Late for us, anyway. When you're old, anything past ten qualifies as late."

Sophie laughed. "You and Mom aren't old. Not at all."

In their early seventies, her parents still had a lot of life to live. She thought of the excellent progress her father had made since his stroke.

If he'd lived a hundred years ago, he'd be dead. Instead, modern medicine had given him an additional, she hoped, good twenty years.

Ned slung an arm around Sophie's shoulders and pressed a kiss against her temple. "Having you here lights up my night."

"I'm sure if you didn't see me, you and Mom would get along just fine." Okay, so maybe that wasn't the most elegant way to probe, but it was the best she could come up with on short notice.

Puzzlement filled her father's eyes. "You know that's not true. You're our girl."

Her father pushed open the door and, as Bentley surged past them, called, "Kris, look who I found skulking out on the sidewalk."

Sophie followed her father into the house and inhaled the enticing scent of freshly baked bread.

Her mother appeared in the doorway leading to the kitchen, her mouth lifting into a smile the second she saw her daughter.

"Sophie." Kris crossed the room to give her a welcoming hug. "We're going simple tonight. Soup, salad and bread."

"A winning combination." Sophie made a great show of inhaling deeply. "The bread smells amazing."

Kris lifted her hands and smiled at her husband. "That's your dad's doing. You know how much he loves baking bread."

"Well, it smells terrific."

"The soup still needs to simmer for a few more minutes. Have a seat." Kris gestured to the comfortable sofa upholstered in a muted floral print. "You look especially lovely this evening."

Sophie glanced down at the simple buttercup-yellow dress. She'd pulled it from her closet because the color made her think of the paper roses...and Josiah.

Kris dropped down on the sofa to sit by her daughter. "Will Dylan also be at this event tonight?"

"We're no longer seeing each other." Sophie kept her tone light. "Before you ask, I feel good about my decision to end our relationship."

She hoped adding that she was cool with it would forestall their questions.

"I'm glad," was all her mother said.

"If you're happy, I'm happy," her dad added.

Sophie's gaze sharpened. It appeared her father had provided the perfect segue to what she wanted to discuss with them this evening. "Do you really mean that?"

Confusion blanketed her father's face. "Mean what?"

"If I'm happy, you're happy."

"Of course I do." Her father paused in his petting of Bentley, who'd jumped onto his lap the second he'd taken a seat in the chair near the sofa.

"What's this about, Sophie?"

She should have expected that her mom would catch the nuances. You didn't spend the majority of your professional life listening to people's problems without picking up on subtext.

"Remember when I told you about my crazy dream?"

"Did you have another?" Kris asked.

"Something like that," Sophie hedged, then chided herself for not spitting out what she needed to say.

"Are you feeling okay?" Worry darkened her father's brown eyes. When he leaned forward, Bentley jumped off his lap.

A second later, the dog's warm body was pressed against Sophie's thigh, his head on her knee. She felt herself steady as she stroked his soft fur.

"I'm feeling good," she assured her parents. "Great, in fact."

The tiny lines around her father's eyes eased, but her mother's gaze remained watchful.

"The new dream—was it the same as before?" Her mother's warm smile and easy tone were at odds with the concern in her eyes.

"I no longer believe that what I experienced was a dream." Sophie continued to stroke Bentley, who emitted soft sounds of bliss.

"What do you think it was?" Kris asked.

"Would anyone like some coffee? Or something else to

drink?" Ned surged to his feet, then smiled at his daughter. "Or perhaps a piece of bread, still warm from the oven?"

"Nothing for me."

"I'll let you and your mom talk this out."

Normally, Sophie would have appreciated the privacy, but what she was about to say concerned him as much as it did her mom.

"Please, Dad, sit. I'd like you to hear this as well."

"Well, okay." Ned resumed his seat in the chair, his gaze now as watchful as his wife's. "What is it, honey?"

"I believe I've been traveling back in time."

The protests were already being voiced when Sophie spoke again, more firmly this time. "I need you to listen. More importantly, I'm asking both of you to keep an open mind."

Then, as she had earlier with Ruby and with Josiah, Sophie laid it out for them.

Her father's face held a look of stunned disbelief.

Her mother, being more experienced at schooling her emotions, looked no more concerned than if Sophie had just announced the sky was blue.

"I believe that this coin," Sophie pulled the love token from her bag and held it out, "is the catalyst."

Her mother took the coin and inspected it carefully, then handed it back without a word.

"It sounds as if you also think the third tent you claim to see—"

"I don't claim to see it, Mom. I see it. It's as clear to me as the other two."

Her mother lifted a hand. "Okay, what I was attempting to say is that it sounds as if both the tent and the Chautauqua play a part."

Sophie nodded.

"Once those are gone, the dreams will likely go away, too."

Sophie started to protest her mother's use of the word *dreams*, but decided to stay on point.

"As will my ability to see Josiah again." Sophie met her mother's gaze. "I fear that once the tents are taken down on Monday after the performances, Josiah will be forever lost to me."

She let out a long breath, suddenly incredibly weary. It had been a long, emotional day filled with more ups and downs than a steeplechase track.

Her gaze shifted from her mother to her dad. "I love you both so much."

She wished they could all be together, but she knew that wasn't possible. But how could she choose? Either way, she would lose contact with people she loved if she went back to 1916 and stayed there.

To her horror, Sophie felt a couple of tears slip down her cheeks. She hurriedly brushed them away.

"Oh, Sophie." Her mother's voice dropped, husky with reassurance. "The mind is an amazing machine. Your deep subconscious must really feel you're ready to branch out if one dream can inspire such strong feelings."

Hadn't her mother listened to anything she'd said?

"It wasn't just one dream." Sophie stopped. Why was she even using the word *dream*? She was traveling through time.

And facing a momentous decision.

Should she stay in 1916 with Josiah, the man she'd quickly come to love, who believed her implicitly?

Or here with the family she loved, who didn't seem to believe her at all?

16

Sophie had just stepped out of her car in front of Charlie and Hannah's house when she spotted Ruby getting out of an Uber.

"I could have given you a ride over," Sophie told her, waiting on the sidewalk.

Ruby waved an airy hand. "I met some friends at the Crab Shack. It would have been out of the way for you."

"Not that far." Sophie forced a light tone. "I wouldn't have minded swinging by and—"

"Dylan was there with his new girlfriend."

"Oh." Sophie inclined her head. "What did he have to say?"

Ruby's eyes widened, and she snorted. "I didn't go over and talk to him."

"Why not?"

A look of stunned disbelief crossed Ruby's face. "Have you forgotten he cheated on you with her?"

"I don't care about that," Sophie admitted. "Who he dates is none of my concern. Don't forget, he'll be in on Monday to pick up the wind chime."

"Why are you reminding me?" Ruby's brows drew together. "Won't you be there?"

How to tell Ruby that she wasn't sure she'd be in this century on Monday... "It's the last day of the Chautauqua."

Ruby's gaze sharpened. "You're seriously considering staying."

Not a question. A statement that required an honest answer.

Sophie nodded. "I'm seriously considering staying."

"Have you thought about what happens if you go back and get the Spanish flu and die?"

"Pleasant thought." Sophie's lips lifted in a wry smile.

"I'm being serious."

"I'm serious, too. There are no guarantees in life. I could be hit by a car tomorrow."

"True, but you have a lot better chance of surviving an illness or accident now than back then."

Sophie couldn't argue with that logic, so she didn't even try.

"Have you even thought about how complicated this is? Like, if you go back and die in the past, does that mean the Sophie I know never exists? And if that's the case, how could you have gone back in the first place? Those questions probably don't even make sense, but I'm new to this time-travel business."

"Ruby, stop." Sophie turned to fully face her friend. "I don't know the answers to those questions, but I don't think there'll be any issues like that since I'd be going so far back. I do know I've never felt love this powerful before. I can't just walk away from Josiah."

"But you can walk away from your best friend?" When Sophie remained silent, Ruby reached over and grasped her hand. She'd never seen her friend so dogged about anything, but then, Ruby was her closest friend. And this wonderful friendship would end if Sophie left.

"Sophie, no. Just, no. I want to support you, I really do, but you need to think about your life here, about all you'd be giving up."

Sophie could think of nothing more to add to what she'd already said.

"What if you go there and then later you decide you want to come back?" Ruby's expression reminded her of a bulldog's. "What would you do then?"

"I don't believe returning will be an option." Sophie cleared her throat. "Which is why this is such a monumental decision."

"There is no decision. You can't go." Ruby raked a hand through her curls as the two women began walking again. "I can't believe I'm talking about this as if we're speaking of you moving to DC or New York."

"When I first told you about Josiah, you were supportive." Sophie tried to hide the hurt, but couldn't quite stop the tremor in her voice. "Now you're not."

"Oh, Soph, it's not that I'm not supportive. When you told me about Josiah, we both thought it was some kind of weird, wonderful dream." Ruby paused as if to gather her thoughts. "I was happy it made you see that Dylan and you weren't meant to be together. That you deserve someone who really makes you happy. But this is—"

Despite Ruby's obvious efforts to control it, her voice rose. Taking a deep breath, she spoke again, more quietly this time. "Your parents, your friends, your business are all here. What is there for you there?"

"Josiah," Sophie said simply. "I want to be with him."

"Welcome."

Sophie jolted. She and Ruby had continued their discussion as they'd climbed the front steps to the porch of the lovely two-story home.

Neither had realized Hannah had opened the door to greet them. She was a pretty woman, with long blond hair, big blue eyes and superb fashion sense, but it was her friendly smile and sunny disposition that made her beautiful.

"Sophie. Ruby. I'm so glad you came." As Hannah's gaze shifted from her to Ruby, Sophie wondered how much she'd heard.

She didn't have to wait long to find out.

Once inside, several women Ruby worked with at Collister College motioned her over, eager to discuss the hot new professor who'd recently joined the faculty.

Sophie glanced around. "Where's Charlie?"

"Over there." Hannah gestured toward where her dark-haired husband was speaking with Dwight Richards, a frequent customer at Timeless Treasures.

Hannah cleared her throat, drawing Sophie's attention back to her. "I heard a little bit of your conversation with Ruby."

"We're fine," Sophie spoke quickly. "Just a friendly difference of opinion."

Hannah stared at Sophie for a moment, her expression unreadable. Eventually, she said, "You might not know this, but before I moved here, I was married. I lost my husband to cancer. I thought my life had ended with his and that I'd never love again." She paused and drew in a breath. "But then after I moved back here... It's hard to explain, but something...magical happened. I can't quite explain it. Really, it's only Charlie who understands." Hannah's gaze drifted to her husband once more before she refocused on Sophie. "I found people who helped me open up my heart again. And I found Charlie. I couldn't be happier."

Sophie thought of what Josiah had said. Like Hannah, he'd thought he'd never love again after losing Daisy.

"I don't know exactly what you and Ruby are arguing about, and I don't mean to butt in, but...I believe there is magic in GraceTown, the kind that can change our lives for the better.

Whatever it is you've experienced, don't be too quick to dismiss it, no matter what others say."

The next morning, Sophie pulled on a white lace petticoat with a cheery yellow ribbon threaded through the eyelet, then topped it with a muslin floral-print dress. Her straw hat with the ring of yellow roses completed the pretty picture.

She stopped downstairs and stepped into her office. After paying the bills Ruby had left on her desk yesterday, she answered important emails and texts and deleted the rest.

"Sophie." Andrew stood in the doorway to her office. Though Sundays were always busy, especially during tourist season, he'd proved more than capable of handling the store alone. "I've been meaning to ask if you'd like me to go through the trunk while I'm working. If I have time, that is."

"Thank you, but I'd prefer you leave the trunk alone for now," she told him. *Will you have time*, she asked herself, *if you go?*

"Got ya." Andrew nodded. "I'll focus on getting the items already sold ready to ship."

"Sounds like a good plan. I'll be out of touch most of the day," she told him. "If you run into any problems or need anything today, Ruby is on call."

"I'll be fine. But thanks for letting me know."

Sophie headed out the door, the love token in the pocket of her dress, the familiar straw hat on her head. Her heart picked up speed as she thought of seeing Josiah again.

Since she was early when she reached the fairgrounds, instead of heading straight to the third tent, she took a stroll.

What if the tent wasn't essential? What if it was simply being near groups dressed in 1916 fashions? Then maybe her trip wouldn't be final at all. Scanning the crowds, she found only one such group. But when she stepped close and then away, nothing happened.

She made her way to the performance area. The third tent was there. Though she was happy that she was in the right place, it appeared that the tent was indeed as critical as the love token.

Would the tent remain once the Chautauqua ended, and the other tents were taken down? There was no way to know for sure until that happened. For now, it appeared Sophie would have to stand by her earlier belief that once the Chautauqua was over, the portal would close.

Sophie barely noticed the quartet on the stage as she hurried to the third tent's back exit.

The instant she stepped through, she saw Josiah waiting for her, hat in hand, an anxious look on his handsome face.

All worry disappeared when he saw her. He crossed the short distance to her in several long strides, took her in his arms and spun her around.

She was laughing when her feet touched the ground.

"You came." His broad smile lit up his face.

"Of course I did." She trailed the tips of her fingers down his handsome cheek. "Did you think I wouldn't?"

"I hoped you would." His gaze swept over her, from her boots to her floral dress the color of buttercups and the familiar straw hat perched on her pinned-up hair. "You look lovely."

"You're looking pretty spiffy yourself."

The shades of blue in his suit only emphasized the blueness of his eyes.

"Thank you." He took her arm. "I'm yours for the day."

"Same here." Happiness filled her at the thought of the entire day stretched before them. "What should we do?"

"The Orioles are playing in Baltimore this afternoon," he

told her. "I have tickets to the game. There will be the drive, of course, but the turnpike is well-maintained, so it should be a pleasant journey."

"I love baseball." Sophie could practically smell the popcorn and peanuts in the air. "I can think of nothing better than spending the day at a ballpark with you."

JOSIAH HAD WORRIED Sophie wouldn't show up. He could admit that now, but only to himself. Not because he didn't trust her, but because if she was traveling through time—which the mere thought made him twitchy—anything could go wrong.

Now here she was laughing, smiling and chattering nonstop as he helped her into his car.

In a few short days, this woman had changed his life. Josiah had planned to spend the rest of his life alone, had told himself that was what he preferred. But Sophie, sweet, funny Sophie, had pulled him back into the world.

He was trying hard not to worry about tomorrow and the end to the Chautauqua festivities. Later, they could talk about that. Right now, he wanted to hear everything that had happened since she'd last left him.

After paying the toll, well worth it in his estimation for a smooth ride to Baltimore, Josiah drove onto the turnpike, his goggles firmly in place to protect his eyes.

"This is a nice road." Sophie shifted in her seat to better face him.

"I don't know if you're familiar with the history, but this turnpike has existed for well over one hundred years." Josiah was pleased that being Sunday, traffic was light, so he didn't have to concentrate totally on the road. "It came about as a way to move goods to and from Baltimore to outlying areas."

"Well, I'm certainly enjoying the smooth ride." Sophie studied the strong lines of his face, now in profile.

Though the short distance to Baltimore would take nearly two hours to drive, considering the slow speed of the Tin Lizzie, Sophie didn't mind. That was two more hours to spend with Josiah.

The day was cloudy, which meant there was no sun to heat up the car. She would have to get used to that, Sophie thought, the lack of so many things she took for granted. "How do you keep your house cool in the summer?"

Her question must have come out of left field to him, because he appeared startled.

"Pardon?"

"During the hottest days, how do you keep your house cool?"

"First, think 'comfortable,' not 'cool.'" He slanted a quick glance in her direction and flashed a smile. "When the temperature soars, it's impossible to keep a house cool. The goal is to keep it comfortable."

"Okay." Sophie settled back in her seat. "How do you keep your house comfortable?"

His brow furrowed in puzzlement. "This is what you want to talk about?"

"Humor me."

"Shade from the trees helps." Josiah thought for a moment. "Outdoor window awnings block the worst of the sun. I also make sure to close any shades and curtains."

Sophie nodded. Even though they used their air conditioner, her parents were all about saving energy. "My mom and dad also close their blinds when it gets really hot."

"I think I'd like your parents."

"They'd like you, too," Sophie agreed, pushing aside the sadness that welled up when she thought about how they would never meet him. "What else?"

"My home has high ceilings, which allows the warm air to rise, and the house was designed to encourage the cooler morning and evening breezes to flow through." Josiah steered around a slight rise in the road. "Of course, I close the windows during the day to keep the cooler air in and the heat out."

"Isn't it difficult to sleep at night?"

"Sometimes." Josiah shrugged. "If it gets too warm, I sleep on the porch."

"The porch?" Sophie's voice rose.

Josiah chuckled. "You'll have to try it sometime."

If she stayed, she might have a chance to have that experience.

"How do you stay cool in the heat?" he asked.

Josiah's question took Sophie by surprise, though she wasn't sure why. If she had questions about how he lived in these times, he was bound to have questions for her about the future.

"The majority of homes have what's called air conditioning." Sophie did her best to explain how the units worked. "Cars have them, too."

"Tell me more about the cars."

He listened intently as she told him about the many features modern cars had, how fast they could go, how some could drive and park themselves.

For a moment, silence filled the interior of the car, a vehicle with only the most basic of features.

She touched his arm. "What are you thinking?"

"I'm wondering how you can even be considering leaving behind that kind of life." The eyes that he settled on her were clear and very blue. "The inventions I marvel at must seem so basic to you."

"It's not the luxuries that make a house a home. And it's not modern conveniences that enrich a life. It's being with someone you love, someone who cares about and for you."

He slowly nodded. "When Daisy died, I couldn't imagine opening my heart to anyone again. I think, deep down, I didn't want to be hurt, to ever grieve for anyone like that again."

"Now?" she prompted when he didn't continue for a moment.

He reached over and took her hand, giving it a fierce squeeze. "I fear that now that I've found that special someone and opened my heart to her, I'm only going to lose her again."

"You're not going to lose me, Josiah." In that moment, Sophie knew she would move heaven and earth to spend the rest of her life with this man. "Because I want to be with you, too."

17

Sophie gazed in wonder as the city of Baltimore came into view. Because they had time before the first pitch, Josiah took her on a drive through the city.

They drove past the brick front of the Old Bay Line terminal where horses and buggies sat side by side with cars. She gazed at the impressive buildings of Baltimore's post office and City Hall and the Washington Monument, all historic structures that Sophie had seen many times on her visits to Baltimore.

She saw Gay Street as a dirt road and smoke billowing from stacks. Dockworkers unloaded bananas from a steamship in the harbor, while in the business district, horses pulled carriages alongside streetcars.

Josiah paused the car in front of the recently completed Baltimore Gas and Electric Company Building.

"It's twenty-one stories tall," Josiah proudly pointed out.

Sophie studied the building with its impressive façade of gray granite and gray-and-white marble. "Is it the tallest one in Baltimore?"

Josiah rubbed his chin, and his expression grew thoughtful.

"I believe my father said something about it being tied with the Emerson Bromo-Seltzer Tower for that honor."

As if a thought had just struck him, he turned to Sophie. "What's the tallest building in Baltimore in your time?"

As she'd spent her college years in Baltimore, Sophie knew the answer. "The Transamerica building in the Inner Harbor is forty stories."

"Nearly twice as tall." Josiah blinked, then took another look at the building in front of them. "What's the tallest in the country?"

"I believe One World Trade Center in New York is about a hundred stories." Sophie opened her mouth to mention how the building had been built after terrorist attacks in 2001 took down the original buildings, but knew that would only prompt more questions.

"Unbelievable." Shaking his head, Josiah pulled away from the curb. "Let's head to the game."

Sophie was enjoying seeing familiar sights and some not-so-familiar ones. Most of all, she enjoyed being with Josiah.

This route to the ballpark was unfamiliar, though.

"I thought we were going to the ballpark."

"This is the way to the ballpark," he told her. At her puzzled look, he added, "Oriole Park."

Oh, right, she thought. The stadium she was familiar with wasn't the same park or even at the same location.

Josiah expelled a breath. "I wish Babe was still pitching for the team. The man was amazing."

Now that Josiah mentioned it, Sophie recalled reading how Babe Ruth had started his pitching career at Baltimore.

The field wasn't at all what Sophie had expected. The bleachers, constructed of wood, were on only one side of the diamond.

"At night during the summer, you can come here and watch

moving-picture shows," Josiah told Sophie, helping her out of the Tin Lizzie. "They have an entire change of programs every evening, and the seats are only ten cents."

"Why would people come here rather than go to the theater?"

He flashed a quick smile. "No air conditioning in the theaters."

Stands outside the stadium sold food and drinks. Sophie smiled when Josiah bought them Cracker Jack to munch on during the game.

The benches were hard, but Sophie didn't mind. The petticoat under her dress provided extra padding.

Josiah studied the players warming up on the diamond. They'd done a lot of talking on the drive from GraceTown, and right now Sophie was content to simply sit by his side and take in the sights, sounds and smells that surrounded her.

What if this became her reality? She would wake up every morning and go to sleep at this man's side every night. It sounded as if his family was close, which was good, because if she became a permanent part of his life, they would be her family, too.

Reveling in the cool breeze brushing against her cheeks, Sophie saw the years stretched before them.

A band formed around her chest and squeezed as she recalled the lessons from her history classes.

World War I. Trench warfare. Artillery shelling. Mustard gas. Spanish influenza.

Ruby's words echoed in her head. What if she died? Worse, what if Josiah did?

It suddenly became difficult for Sophie to breathe. Though the pitcher appeared ready to take the mound, Sophie closed her fingers around Josiah's coat jacket.

The smile on his face faded when he turned to her and saw

her face. "What's wrong?"

"Promise me something."

His gaze never left her face. "Anything."

"In two years, there is going to be an influenza pandemic." She kept her gaze focused on him, trying to will him to see how serious she was. "Fifty million people will die worldwide, including almost seven hundred thousand Americans. There is no treatment."

The grip she had on his coat sleeve tightened. "It's a virus, a germ that you can't see. It's spread by breathing the same air as someone who is ill. People cough. People sneeze. Which is why you'll need to isolate yourself and your family when it starts and keep isolating. The government will tell you not to worry, but it's very dangerous, and another wave will come in 1919. It cannot be business as usual. Not if you want to survive."

Concern furrowed Josiah's brow. "That sounds awful."

"It will be. As will the stock market crash in 1929. For you, it's the future. For me, it's history."

"It can't be all bad in the future."

"No, of course not," Sophie hastened to assure him. "There are so many wonderful inventions that make life easier and better, as well as amazing advances in medical diagnosis and treatment."

Something flickered in his eyes. "In the future, would my Daisy have survived the infection that took her life?"

"It's still serious to have a ruptured appendix." Sophie thought of the little boy in her fifth-grade class who'd had that happen when his parents had brushed off his complaints of pain. "But there are drugs in my time called antibiotics that likely would have helped."

Sorrow blanketed his face.

Releasing her hold on his arm, Sophie chided herself for ruining what until now had been a lovely day.

Gently, Josiah reached over and took her hand in his. "I imagine there are dozens of cures on the horizon that could help people who live here now, but we're simply not there yet. That's not your fault, Sophie." He offered a smile. "We might not be able to change the world, but we can live every moment, enjoying the time we have."

The crack of a bat hitting a ball had everyone jumping up and cheering. Sophie and Josiah rose to their feet. When she brought two fingers to her lips and whistled the way her dad had taught her, Josiah grinned.

For the rest of the afternoon, Sophie kept the conversation focused on baseball. By the time they left the stands, with a win for the Orioles, the haunted look had left Josiah's eyes.

"Are you ready to return to GraceTown?" Before she could respond, he added, "If you have time once we get back, I'd love to show you my house."

She smiled. "I'd love to see it."

When they reached the car, he opened the door with a flourish, bowing deeply. "Your chariot, ma'am."

She laughed, and warmth rushed through her. Sophie liked how he was able to be serious when the situation dictated, but how he didn't let things he could do nothing about bring him down.

Though she knew Josiah had taken her warning about the upcoming pandemic to heart, he'd been able to set those worries aside so they could enjoy their time together.

"Thank you," she said when he slid behind the wheel.

"For what?"

"For being you." She lifted her shoulders and let them drop. "You're a wonderful man, Josiah Huston, and I'm proud to be with you today."

~

Sophie had discovered that riding in a car without windows was a lot like being a passenger in a convertible—the wind could be brutal. Thankfully, she found a band in her purse and used it to tie back her hair.

Though she wasn't sure when sunglasses came into widespread use, she pulled a pair from her bottomless purse and put them on. Instantly, she felt better.

Once they were back in town, Sophie took the time to look around. Josiah stayed on the main roadway until finally turning onto a residential street.

He drove slowly up and down the streets, giving her time to take in the various neighborhoods that made up GraceTown at the turn of the twentieth century. Some of these areas were familiar to Sophie, while areas like where her parents lived now had not yet been developed.

She found herself relaxing, and despite the wind whipping tendrils of hair into her face, she couldn't imagine anything better than riding in a Model T with Josiah.

Each time he slanted a glance in her direction and smiled, her heart skipped a beat.

No, there was nowhere else she'd rather be.

She had to admit there would be advantages to living in a time that wasn't so busy, where a person could simply enjoy laughter and conversations with friends without being constantly interrupted by texts and tweets and breaking-news alerts.

Still, Sophie realized that her desire to stay had more to do with Josiah, about being with a person she felt connected to, who was interested in and curious about the same things she was. For all the times her parents or Ruby encouraged her to cultivate the life and love she truly wanted, this was the first time she understood what they'd been trying to tell her.

As they drove farther into town, Sophie realized the houses

were gradually becoming larger. In this area, homes sat back from the street with lawns like thick blankets of green spread out in front of them.

She noticed the houses had been strategically located to take advantage of existing trees that blocked the sun from heating a home's interior. Many of the houses also sported awnings, and those that didn't had the shades drawn or curtains pulled.

It was a gorgeous area, where porches sported flowerpots of brightly colored blooms, and nearly every driveway had a vehicle parked next to the house.

The street itself was constructed of bricks, which somehow only added to the warmth of the surroundings.

Sophie was about to ask Josiah if he was acquainted with anyone who lived in this neighborhood when he pulled to a stop in front of an impressive three-story brick residence.

Was this beauty, with its tall windows, wraparound porch and cupula, his home?

He took off his goggles and looked at her. His dark hair was mussed from the wind, which served to give him a boyish appearance. "This is it."

She turned her gaze to him and smiled. "It's gorgeous."

"I'm happy you like it." Rounding the front of the vehicle, he opened her door and took her hand as she stepped out.

Sophie inhaled the clean, fresh scent of him. "You smell good."

A look of startled surprise crossed his face, then he grinned. "My shaving soap."

She looped her arm through his. "Don't stop using it."

As they strode to the steps of the front porch, he smiled down at her. "Being with you makes me happy."

Tightening her hold on his bicep, she looked up at him. Her heart skipped a beat at the look in his eyes. "It's the same for me."

When Josiah reached the door, he turned briefly.

Sophie did the same, just in time to see the curtains at the front window of the home across the street drop back into place.

"My neighbor, Mrs. Abernathy, is interested in neighborhood activities." He spoke in a matter-of-fact tone and motioned her inside.

"She'll likely gossip about seeing me here with you."

"Likely."

Since that fact didn't appear to bother him, she stepped into the spacious home. It struck her that if they married, this would be her home.

Sophie blinked at the sight of shiny hardwood floors, an attractive rug and lots of ornate wood on a stairway leading to the second floor.

"Is this the home you lived in with Daisy?" she asked conversationally.

"Yes." His gaze searched hers. "Though she passed away at the hospital in Baltimore, this is where we lived since moving to GraceTown. Would it bother—?"

"I'd be proud to call this my home."

"I loved it from the moment I first saw it," Josiah admitted. "Many of the Victorian homes along this avenue have detailed trim and gingerbread. This house, on the other hand, was constructed in 1907, and the design of homes had become more restrained then."

As Sophie's gaze drifted out the window, she envisioned herself sitting on the porch with Josiah in the months and years to come.

Her gaze returned to the spacious parlor. They would build a life and make a home together. She wasn't sure what she would do for work in the early twentieth century, but she felt confident she could find something that she would enjoy and that would give her satisfaction.

Then, when they had children—

She glanced at Josiah. "Do you want children?"

He inclined his head.

"You mentioned once that you and Daisy weren't blessed. Was that because—?"

"Daisy had some female issues." Josiah gestured toward the stairs. "This home has four bedrooms and room for more on the third level. I would be happy to fill every room with children."

"You'd be a good dad."

He reached for her hand. "We'd be good parents together." His fingers closed around hers. "Sophie, I don't know if I can express how much you've changed my life in these few short days. I thought the possibility of a home and a family of my own were behind me. I wanted them behind me. I thought by closing myself off, I could stay in control and safeguard myself against more unexpected grief. Then you came along, and I can say that nothing in my life has ever been so unexpected."

Sophie laughed. "Are you calling me grief?" she teased.

"No! Quite the opposite. You, my Sophie, are pure joy. You remind me how good it feels to share moments with someone. If I can be brave enough to open my mind to a woman from the future, then surely I can be brave enough to open my heart up to love."

"I'd never been in love...before you. I had started to wonder if I was incapable of loving someone as deeply as, say, my mother loves my father. But you, being with you... Well, it's shown me what true love feels like."

His gaze met hers. "I don't know what I'd do if I lost you."

Reaching over, she squeezed his hand. "One thing we've both learned is that life doesn't come with guarantees. But I believe you and I were meant to find each other, and I'm going to do everything I can to make sure nothing tears us apart."

18

When Josiah had asked if she'd like the grand tour of his home, she'd jumped at the chance.

They started in the parlor, with its ornate crown molding, terra cotta paint and polished maple floors. "This room has such a warm, welcoming feel."

She saw by his smile that her comment pleased him. Sophie was about to ask about the gramophone perched on an ornate table near the window when he motioned her into the kitchen.

She marveled at the stove with its clear front and the electric refrigerator. Her research into 1916 had shown her that owning these two appliances wasn't the norm for this era.

As if noticing her admiring glances, Jonah pointed. "That is a Kelvinator electric refrigerator, and that is a Boss glass-door oven."

"The latest and greatest." Sophie smiled up at him.

"When I purchased this house, I made it clear that I wanted the kitchen updated with all the modern conveniences. Although it was only five years old at the time, there have been many advances in the last fifteen years. The appliances are also the most modern." Pride filled Josiah's voice. He gestured with his hand toward a stainless-steel coffeepot on the counter. "This percolator is something I would now find difficult to do without."

Sophie smiled, thinking of the elaborate coffee machine sitting on the counter in her apartment. How many times had she told Ruby that she simply couldn't live without it?

But when Josiah's arms slid around her, Sophie knew that a percolator would be just fine.

The bathroom, with its beautiful black and white tile in a hexagon pattern, would have been lovely in a modern home. She eyed the deep claw-foot tub, already imagining soaking in bubbles up to her chin. She marveled at the needle-nose shower that sprayed water from all sides, but then studied the counterless sink and wondered where a woman would keep all her toiletries.

"Let me show you the second floor. Hold on to the rail. The stairs are steep." He followed her up the stairs to the second level. They stood for a moment in the hallway, the wood floors gleaming, the scent of lemon polish in the air.

Sophie sniffed. This house was not only beautiful but spotless. "Do you have someone in to clean?"

He nodded. "Mrs. Wessel, my housekeeper, cleans and prepares meals."

"Well, if the cleanliness of your house is any indication, she's a gem. You need to keep that woman on your payroll."

The tense set to Josiah's shoulders eased. "She's a widow and is grateful for the income."

It didn't surprise Sophie that helping someone would please Josiah.

"There are four bedrooms."

A quick tour showed three of the bedrooms were minimally furnished, with only a bed covered by a quilt and a bedside stand.

The fourth bedroom was larger than the others and sported a fireplace with a blue tile frontage and built-in bookcases on both sides. The bed frame boasted a brass bisque iron finish with a curvature at the top of the headboard and footboard.

Josiah pushed a button just inside the door, and the lights came on.

Sophie turned to Josiah. “Not many homes have electric power in 1916.”

“That is true.” He smiled. “This is my room.”

“As if I couldn’t tell.” Sophie nudged him with her elbow, her tone teasing.

He inclined his head, his expression puzzled.

Sophie gestured wide with one hand. “It’s the biggest room with the largest bed, the most furnishings and a fireplace.”

“We were going to do more with the other rooms once we had the time, but...”

“It’s lovely. This room is lovely. And this bed,” Sophie moved to it and slid her hand across the top of the quilt, “looks so comfortable.”

When she looked up, she found Josiah staring. The heat in eyes had her ready to cross the room and demand—just thinking the word made her smile—that he make love to her, but then he turned on his heels and headed down the stairs.

She was left with no choice but to follow.

When she reached the bottom of the steps, she found him standing in the parlor, staring out the front window.

Sophie started toward him, but was distracted by the gramophone she’d noticed earlier. She shifted course to inspect the player more closely. She noted the turntable contained a phonograph record.

As it had only moments earlier, when she glanced up and caught Josiah staring, the longing in his eyes had blood flowing through her veins like warm honey. She cleared her throat. "What were you listening to?"

Sophie wasn't sure what to think when he shifted uncomfortably from one foot to the other.

"WC Handy's 'Memphis Blues.'" Josiah cleared his throat. "It is thought that Vernon Castle liked the rhythm and used it to create the bunny hug dance."

Daisy loved them all, especially the...bunny hug.

Josiah held out a hand. "I hope that you understand—"

Sophie closed his lips with her fingers. "Daisy was your wife. You have many happy memories. I get that. I also understand that it's only natural you'd want to revisit them every now and again."

Relief crossed his face at her understanding words.

Sophie smiled brightly. "Show me how it's done."

Josiah blinked. "Pardon?"

"The bunny hug."

A slow smile spread across his lips. "You want to dance the bunny hug?"

"I do."

He started the gramophone by turning the crank. The tinny sound of the blues filled the air. Once the music started, Josiah turned to her. "We start by being cheek to cheek."

Sophie flashed a smile. "I'm liking this dance already."

But when she pressed her cheek to his and encircled his neck with her arms, he chuckled and unwrapped her arms. "Not like that, I'm afraid."

Heaving a long-suffering sigh, she placed her cheek against his and kept her body back. "Do we have to keep our hands to ourselves?"

He smiled.

"Mine go around you to rest on your back." He illustrated. "You place your hands on my shoulders."

They quickly achieved the appropriate stance. It took Sophie only a second to realize that, in many ways, this was a far more intimate stance than if they'd been wrapped around each other in a tight embrace.

His lips were so close she could feel his warm breath against her cheek, and the enticing scent of his soap teased her nostrils. All she'd need to do was turn her head a fraction of an inch, and her mouth would be on his.

His fingers on her back seemed incredibly sensual, even though a layer of clothing separated them from her bare skin.

Sophie found even the light touch of her hands on his broad shoulders stirred her senses.

The fact that his body, that hard, well-toned body, was kept just out of reach teased and tantalized. In that instant, Sophie understood why this simple dance was considered scandalous.

"I move eight steps forward." Josiah's deep voice cut through her fog of desire. "You move back eight steps."

At five steps back, Sophie had reached her breaking point. Forget keeping her distance. She did what she'd been wanting to do all afternoon.

Flinging her arms around Josiah's neck, she turned her head and kissed him full on the lips.

Surprise had him opening his mouth, just a little.

Sophie took advantage and immediately deepened the kiss.

She couldn't get enough of him.

Need warred with propriety as she slid her fingers into his hair, pressing herself tightly against him, reveling in the evidence of his desire for her.

Tilting her head back, she gazed up at him. "Josiah."

A single word imbued with a question.

Will you make love to me?

"Sophie." Placing his hands on her hips, he pulled her closer to him. "I want you so badly."

Heart hammering in her chest, she planted a moist kiss on his neck, loving the salty taste of him. "I want you double as much."

"Not possible." He chuckled softly, then his expression turned serious. "You and I—"

"We love each other." Sophie knew the mores of the time and the battle that likely waged inside him. She also knew the rightness of this.

"I want to marry you. To make you my wife. To spend the rest of my life making you happy." His words came out in a rush. "I want to propose to you under the stars with a bouquet of yellow roses and pretty words that let you know you have my heart. I—"

Her fingers to his lips stopped whatever else he was about to say. "You can still do all that. But right now, I want to go upstairs to your bedroom and make love with you."

The kiss he gave in answer was long, slow and deep, and her head was spinning by the time they broke apart.

But when she started toward the stairs, Josiah placed a staying hand on her arm. "Not today."

Turning back, she stared at him in disbelief. "You...you... don't want me?"

He grazed her cheek with his knuckles, his eyes filled with such tenderness and love, her heart swelled. "I want you more than breath."

"Then why—?"

"Because, my sweet Sophia, we will do this right." He must have seen her continued confusion, because he spoke without waiting for her response. "I will get a ring. Then I will bring you a bouquet of yellow roses and get down on one knee and ask you to be my wife. If your father were here, I would ask for his blessing."

"We don't need to wait for any of that. We—"

"I know some do not, but I was raised to be an honorable man. We will marry, then I will take you to my bed. Not before."

The finality in his tone told Sophie there was no use arguing. She could not, would not push or tempt him to defy his personal standards. "I understand."

"I knew you would."

"At least tell me you want me as much as I want you."

Josiah chuckled. "Oh, my darling Sophie, you have no idea how much I want you. But very soon, assuming you accept my proposal, we shall be together forever."

"Have no doubt as to my answer, Josiah." Sophie offered him an impish smile. "But, because you are making me wait, I'll make you wait for my answer until you are on your knee, and the ring is in your hand."

For over an hour, Sophie relaxed with Josiah on the porch of his home. They were there so long the ornate lights at the edge of the street winked on.

With a regretful sigh, Sophie pushed to her feet. "I suppose I should be getting back to the fairgrounds."

Josiah slowly rose, then moved to her, wrapping his hands around her forearms. "Don't go back. Stay here with me. Build a life with me. I promise that I will do everything in my power to make you happy."

Temptation surged, and Sophie was on the verge of agreeing. Then she thought of her parents. And Ruby. She needed to say proper good-byes. She also needed to make plans for Timeless Treasures.

She couldn't simply disappear and leave those she loved to handle the fallout.

Not caring about Josiah's nosy neighbor, she wrapped her

arms around him and laid her head against his chest. "I need to go back at least one more time."

"I can't help but worry that if you return to your time tonight, you might never come back." As he spoke, his palm gently stroked the back of her head.

"The Chautauqua event doesn't end until tomorrow," she reminded him.

"Before Daisy's surgery, the doctor told me not to worry. He assured me that he'd done that operation a hundred times. He would take out her appendix, and she would be back home with me soon."

"He didn't know it had already ruptured."

"No, he did not," Josiah agreed, walking with her to the Model T. "It was an unforeseen circumstance that changed everything."

"You're right. There are no guarantees in life. I could be struck by a car and die. The same could happen to you. But these are things that aren't likely to happen." Sophie lifted pleading eyes to his. "I don't want to leave you. I wish with every atom of my being that I could simply stay here and start to build a life with you from this moment forward."

"But you won't."

"I can't." She rested the palm of her hand against his cheek. "I have to say a proper good-bye to my parents and to my friend. I have to make plans for the store I own. Until that is done, I can't embrace a new life with you."

"I understand." Josiah blew out a breath and raked a hand through his hair. "In your place, I'd want to do the same."

"Trust me, Josiah," Sophie told him. "Trust me to come back to you."

19

Josiah did trust Sophie, but when they reached the fairgrounds, he was tempted to hold her tightly against him and not let her go. All the worst scenarios kept circling through his head.

To his surprise, instead of throwing open the door and stepping out, a task she was more than capable of performing on her own, Sophie remained where she was, a pensive look on her face.

"I don't want you to go, to take that risk." Josiah shifted to face her, and even he heard the worry in his voice. "Stay with me. Be my wife. I promise I'll spend the rest of my life making you happy."

"Soon. Soon, we'll be together." She cupped his face with her hand and kissed him gently on the lips. "Don't worry. I'll make it back."

Was it only his imagination, or was her smile a little wobbly? Was that concern in her hazel depths that she was trying hard not to let him see?

"You're worried, too."

After a long moment, she gave a nod. "Just a little. I think that it's because I want this so much. If I didn't, it wouldn't matter. I'd simply go back to my old life if things didn't work out for some reason."

"Now?" The word was all he could push past his suddenly frozen lips.

"Now," she sighed the word, "while I know that we both would go on, not seeing you again would leave a gaping hole in my heart, one that I'm not sure could ever be filled."

Josiah knew how that gaping hole felt, and he wouldn't want anyone to experience that pain, especially the woman he loved.

"If something goes wrong—" he began.

"Nothing will—"

"If something goes wrong," he said as if she hadn't spoken, "I want you to promise me something."

Tears glistened at the edges of her lashes. "Nothing is going to go wrong."

The distress in her voice had him reaching out and stroking a palm down her soft curls. "If it does."

She lifted hazel eyes glistening with tears to his.

He steadied himself against the sudden stabbing pain in the area of his heart that the mere thought of never seeing her again evoked. "If it does, I want you to move forward with your life and be happy."

"How can I do that?" she cried, drawing the attention of several couples passing by. Her voice lowered. "How can I do that without you? I've waited my whole life for you, and the thought of not being with you is...horrific."

"I understand." He forced his voice to steady. "It's—"

"I know you understand. It breaks my heart that you do." She swiped at her eyes and sniffled.

Reaching into his pocket, he pulled out a freshly pressed handkerchief and held it out. "Here."

Offering him a grateful look, she took it, wiped her eyes,

then blew her nose. "I love you so much. Until you, I didn't have anyone who even came close to touching my heart. I can't imagine feeling for anyone else what I do for you."

"Let's go for a walk," he suggested. "I realize you need to get back, but we still have some time."

In a minute, they were walking the fairgrounds under a large yellow moon and the glow of incandescent lamps.

"I hope that we never need discover again what life is like without each other." Josiah took her hand, finding her fingers ice-cold despite the warmth of the evening air. "But if we do, we will survive."

She gave her head a shake. "I can't imagine life without you."

"I will always be with you in your heart, and you, my sweet, darling Sophie, will always be with me."

"You think I'm not coming back," she accused. "That's why you're saying all this, because you don't think I'm coming back." Her voice rose and broke.

Josiah took a deep breath. "I know you will do whatever you can to come back. If I didn't believe that..." He shook his head, not sure what to say as emotion rose up and seemed to squeeze his chest in a vise. "All I'm saying is that I love you, and whether we're together or apart, you will be with me here..." Josiah placed a hand over his heart. "Always."

After several long heartbeats, Sophie gave a jerky nod. "You'll be with me always, too."

Then she flung her arms around his neck and held on as if this was the last time they would be together.

Not the last time, Josiah assured himself as he buried his face in her hair and fought the urge to weep. She would come back, and they would be together then.

She would be his wife. He would be her husband. They would fill his silent home with children and laughter. Whatever he could do to make her happy in his world, he would do it.

Tomorrow. When she came back.

With the coin tucked securely in her pocket, Sophie clutched Josiah's hands and studied his face one last time, memorizing every feature. "I'll be back. Tomorrow, we will start our new life together."

Bending close, he brushed a chaste kiss across her lips, then straightened. "Safe travels, my love."

With a strength she hadn't known she possessed and hoping she wasn't making the biggest mistake of her life, Sophie stepped into the shed.

She was back to her time in a flash. Though the ease of the transition should have reassured her, fear still lived in Sophie's heart.

She knew it would remain there until she was back in Josiah's arms.

Timeless Treasures was closed when Sophie arrived. She took time wandering the aisles, touching items she remembered purchasing and ones that were her favorites.

Memories of the regular customers she loved visiting with washed over her. She thought of Ruby and Andrew and how much fun the three of them had working together.

She considered calling her mom and dad, but since it was after ten, they were likely already in bed. Still, rarely a day went by when she didn't talk with one of them.

After a moment's consideration, she sent her mom a nonringing message.

Hey, guys, I got home late, so that's why I didn't call. Just wanted to say I love you both very much. You are the best parents a girl could ever have.

Sophie considered saying more...but really, what more was there to say? Still, was this enough for two people who had always been there for her, two people she loved with her whole heart?

She set down her phone, contemplating whether to call Ruby. Ruby didn't agree that she should go back to 1916 to stay. Normally, she and her bestie were on the same page. They'd been at odds the last time they'd spoken. Could she really just leave and not make things right between them?

Maybe she should go back and tell Josiah she couldn't stay with him. Then, at least, he'd know she was safe.

But she loved Josiah and wanted to be with him. Forever.

Sophie's thoughts returned to Ruby, then back to her parents.

Can I really do this? Leave everyone I love behind?

When Sophie stepped out her back door the next morning, she found Ruby waiting.

Her friend leaned against her car and studied Sophie and her small duffel. "You packed light."

Sophie's heart gave a leap at the sight of her friend. "What are you doing here?"

"I know we argued, but if you're really gonna do this, I'm going to see you off."

Sophie wasn't sure what to think. While she was processing, Ruby strode over and tossed her bag into the back of her Jeep. "Get in."

They'd barely gone a mile when Sophie turned to her friend. "Are you here to try to talk me out of this?"

Ruby slanted a glance at her. "Is that a possibility?"

"I was up all night trying to figure out the best way to handle things."

"Well, what have you decided?"

"I'm not sure. I have to believe that when I get there, I'll know what to do."

"All right, well, if you've been up all night, you shouldn't be driving, so it's a good thing I stopped by."

"I've never had to make a decision like this before."

"It's a big one," Ruby agreed.

"I have to trust that, in my heart of hearts, I'll know what to do."

SOPHIE INSISTED Ruby drop her off at the entrance to the fairgrounds. She gave her friend a hug.

"Is this good-bye forever?" Ruby asked, tears shimmering in her chocolate-brown eyes.

"I don't know." Sophie blinked back her own tears and started walking, the duffel slung over her shoulder.

Later today, when the last performances were over, a crew would begin taking down the tents. Though Sophie couldn't be certain, everything in her said that once those tents came down, the third one would vanish forever.

She wasn't worried. By then, she would be with Josiah. And what she needed to do would be clear.

With each step closer to the area where the tents were set up, her heart rate increased.

Nothing would go wrong, she told herself.

Nothing *could* go wrong. If it did, she would never see Josiah again.

The wind had picked up, and thunder rumbled in the

distance. The fact that a storm was moving in barely registered with her. By the time the rain came—and rain was a frequent visitor to GraceTown in August—she would be gone.

She wondered if the weather would be the same today in 1916. Or were the modern-day temperature fluctuations the area had been experiencing the last five years due to climate change?

No matter. The thought of sitting inside with Josiah while the rain fell outside had a rush of warmth coursing through her. If it ended up being a lovely day, perhaps they could sit on his porch again, this time with glasses of lemonade or iced tea.

She enjoyed simply being with him. They didn't have to be doing something every minute of every day for her to be happy. She just needed to be with him. Which was why she believed if she stayed in 1916, she would have little difficulty adjusting to the slower pace.

Yes, she was going to enjoy spending time with him on that lovely porch.

The blue paint on the ceiling had intrigued her, and last night, once she'd finished all her tasks and sleep had still proved elusive, she'd looked it up on her phone.

The color, known as haint blue, represented water. Folklore said spirits couldn't traverse water, so the color was meant to keep them away. Even if you didn't believe that, the color was bright and evoked thoughts of nature and the sky.

She wondered if Josiah had had the porch ceiling painted that color, or had it already been there when he'd purchased the home? Did he subscribe to the whole warding-off-evil-spirits thing?

If she stayed, there would be so much still to learn and discover about him.

Sophie's lips curved as she let her gaze scan the grounds. Though she would likely come to this spot in the future, it would look different. The same way that when she watched the

Orioles play in 1916, it would be at Oriole Park V and not at Camden Yards.

The thought of leaving technology and the world as she knew it behind didn't cause the slightest twinge of regret or sorrow. The only thing that tugged at her heart was leaving her parents and Ruby.

Her mother had assured her that she and her father would be okay, that as much as they would miss her, it would make them happy to know she had a wonderful life with a man she loved.

She knew her mom truly wanted her to be happy, but letting go of someone you loved didn't come easily.

Sophie thought of Josiah waiting for her in 1916. It reminded her of those illustrations she'd seen of heaven, where those on the one shore were weeping and saying, "There she goes," while others on the far shore were dancing up and down and saying, "Here she comes."

Though she couldn't see him jumping up and down, the thought of the smile that would be on Josiah's face when she walked out of the tent today had her practically skipping the last few feet.

She stopped short. Workers had already taken down one tent, and only the poles remained of the other one.

Spotting Alcidean headed to the administration building, Sophie raced over to her. "What's happening?"

Alcidean's brow furrowed in confusion. "What do you mean?"

Sophie gestured in the direction where the tents had once sat, her movement jerky and frantic. "They're taking down the tents."

"Yes, the Chautauqua is over." Alcidean smiled. "It was a huge success, but I have to say I'm ready to relax. Thank you again for volunteering."

"I thought the performances went through today."

"Thursday to Monday. Or, more accurately, Thursday *through* Sunday." Alcidean shook her head. "Today is strike day."

"What? No! That can't be right." Sophie's heart began to beat rapidly.

Alcidean's expression shifted between puzzled and concerned. "Sophie, are you all right?"

Taking in a calming breath, Sophie forced herself to smile. "Yes I...I just...I misunderstood." Without saying another word, Sophie turned and strode back toward the tents. Or rather, where the tents had once been.

Perhaps the love token could still get her back.

Her heart picked up speed again. With all the thoughts and emotions running through her mind that morning, she couldn't recall picking up the love token, much less putting it in her pocket, along with Josiah's handkerchief.

No. No. No.

She could not have left it in her apartment.

With her heart in her throat, Sophie slid her fingers into her pocket.

The tips of her fingers touched the softness of Josiah's handkerchief and nothing else. For a second, she forgot how to breathe, and the heat of the day closed in around her.

Then she touched something hard. The love token.

She swayed as relief flooded her. She pulled it from her pocket. As if it had been waiting for just such a moment, the sun burst through the clouds and cast light on the coin.

Sophie couldn't say for sure what happened next. One second, she was gazing at the coin in her palm. The next second, a group of workmen, laughing and jostling one another as if they were boys and not full-grown men, strode past her.

When the smallest of the four flung out his arms as he talked, his hand hit her outstretched one.

The love token went flying.

The young man called over his shoulder, "Sorry," as he continued walking with his companions.

For a second, just one second, Sophie's gaze shifted to the young man. Then she glanced down, expecting to see the coin at her feet.

It wasn't there. She swept her gaze farther out, but she still didn't see it.

Her heart began to pound an erratic rhythm as she dropped to her knees, ignoring the dust as she frantically searched for the coin.

The love token had to be here. It had to be here. Yes, it had gone flying, but it couldn't have gone far.

Twenty minutes passed, and she was still searching when Alcidean strolled up.

"Sophie. What are you still doing here?" The woman hurried to her side. "What's wrong?"

"I have this special coin. It, ah, it means the world to me."

Concern blanketed Alcidean's face. "I can see that."

"I had it in my hand, and a man bumped into me." Sophie swiped at her eyes. "The coin went flying. I can't find it. I've looked everywhere, but I can't find it."

"Maybe a pair of fresh eyes will help." Alcidean patted her shoulder. "Is it gold or silver?"

"What?"

"The coin. Is it gold or silver?"

"It's gold," Sophie told her.

"We'll find it."

They were still looking when a crew of men appeared and began pulling the tent poles from the ground.

Panic spurted. Sophie grabbed Alcidean's arm. "They can't take down the poles. Tell them to wait."

"Honey." Alcidean pried Sophie's fingers from her arm. "I can't stop them. They don't answer to me."

The tears began falling in earnest now. Josiah was lost to her. Forever lost.

"You don't look so good." Alcidean took Sophie's arm and led her into the shade. "Maybe someone in town has a metal detector you can borrow to help you find the coin."

"It won't matter then." Sophie rested her back against the broad trunk of the tree, a hollow space where her heart had once been. "It will be too late. It's already too late"

SOPHIE WAITED until all the poles were down before making her way to the fairgrounds exit. It had been like watching a body being lowered into the ground at a cemetery. At that point, there was no denying the person you loved was lost to you.

When she reached the exit, she dropped down on a bench and gave in to her grief, crying until there were no more tears left to fall. She imagined Josiah waiting for her, so excited and eager to start their new life together. Then, as time dragged on and she didn't appear, worry would grip him. Not only worry over if she was coming, but fear that something had happened to her in the transition.

Sophie had known worry and fear when her father had been so ill. But this, this all-consuming pain of loss, was different.

She'd never believed a heart could actually break, but the pain in her chest, the overwhelming pressure, was very real.

Maybe she was having a heart attack. Perhaps she should go to the emergency room and get checked out. The fact was, she didn't care if she was. She simply didn't care.

She and Josiah would never be together again. And worse,

the sweet, gentle man who'd opened his heart to her would spend the rest of his life wondering what had happened to her.

When sobs once again consumed her, Sophie realized she'd been wrong. She did have more tears.

Resting her forehead against her hands, she realized something else. A day that had dawned filled with so much promise had turned out to be the worst of her life.

Silently, Josiah watched the workers take down the tents. He knew that since Sophie hadn't arrived by now, she wasn't coming, but he hadn't been able to walk away.

He'd held on to hope as long as he could, but told himself it was time to let go. Let her go.

Josiah turned to do just that when he saw it.

A flash of gold in the dirt.

In several long strides, he was there, scooping up the gold coin.

Could this be Sophie's love token?

Flipping it over to be sure, he read the words. *Love Be Yours, Love Be Mine.*

Closing his eyes for a second, he felt himself steady.

Then he placed it into his pocket and strode off without looking back.

20

O*ne month later*

Sophie pushed open the lid of the steamer trunk and told herself it was time to get to work and inventory the contents. Ever since the day at the fairgrounds, she'd been simply going through the motions at the store.

When she'd returned that day, Ruby had been thrilled to see her and had begun firing all sorts of questions at her. Until she'd seen Sophie's face.

Even now, four weeks later, Sophie had told her friend only that she'd lost the coin, so she had been unable to join Josiah. Was there really anything more to say?

She'd called her mother and told her the same, but then had started crying and had had to end the call. Though she'd spent time with her parents since, Sophie still found it difficult to speak of her grief.

Her pain remained a raw open wound, one she was convinced would never heal.

The thought made her think of Josiah and how he must have felt after Daisy's death. She'd thought she'd understood the pain that had caused him to vow to never love again. She hadn't.

"Ah, Sophie." Andrew cleared his throat. "If you're not up to doing this today, we got a shipment of—"

"The trunk is taking up valuable space." Sophie forced herself to concentrate on the task at hand.

One day at a time. That's how she would get through this.

Still, her heart pinched when she saw the red velvet pouch in Andrew's hand.

"Just set that aside," she told Andrew. "Put it on top of the hatbox of photographs. Those will take me a while to go through and determine what we might be able to sell."

The thought of a lifetime of photographic memories being reduced to what would sell on vintage websites brought Sophie's mood even lower. She still couldn't believe that a family would toss them out like yesterday's trash.

She could only hope they had gone through them, and these were duplicates or ones no one had wanted.

Andrew gave a low whistle. "Well, what do we have here?"

The whistle, along with something in Andrew's tone, had Sophie turning from the dress she was carefully folding. She blinked. "What is that?"

She'd never seen money in quite that quantity.

"I'd say it's a wad o' cash." Andrew flipped through the bills, held together by a rubber band that looked as if it could snap at any moment. "Some of these are Benjamins. There must be thousands of dollars here."

If there were hundred-dollar bills in the wad of cash, Sophie knew Andrew's assessment of the amount was likely spot-on. She held out her hand.

"I'd like to say finders keepers, but you're the boss, and you're the one who bought the trunk and its contents." Andrew grinned and, with a melodramatic show of reluctance, handed over the cash. "You sure got a heckuva deal when you bid on this one."

"I'll be putting the money in the safe—"

"Smart—"

"Then I'm going to call the woman who handled the auction for the estate so we can get this back to the family."

Andrew blinked, surprise skittering across his handsome face. "Give it back? Why? You bought the trunk and everything in it fair and square."

"I doubt whoever put this in with the estate's offerings knew that this amount of money was in the trunk."

"You're seriously going to call the family?" Disbelief had his voice pitching high.

"I seriously am." Sophie studied the rest of the trunk's contents—what she could see, that was. "They may want the entire trunk back. Let's put back what we've taken out until we know for sure."

Andrew heaved an exaggerated sigh. "Why do I feel as if I had a fortune only to have it slip from my hands?"

Sophie thought of Josiah. "I know the feeling."

SOPHIE DIDN'T HAVE to wait long to hear back on the steamer trunk. Apparently, the trunk had been added to the auction in error, and the Wexman family definitely wanted it and its contents back. She was informed that Joe Wexman would be by in the next few days to pick it up.

"They're at least going to pay you back what you bid," Ruby said when Sophie told her and Andrew about the plan.

"I don't know," Sophie said. "If he does, I'm fine with it. If not, that's okay, too."

Though both Ruby and Andrew protested, one look from Sophie told them there was no changing her mind. What Sophie didn't tell them was that even if she'd paid ten thousand dollars for the trunk and now had to lose that amount, it would be worth it.

The trunk had given her the coin, which had given her Josiah.

During the past month, Sophie had fought to find the good in what had happened to her. She realized that she'd been forever changed by meeting Josiah. Family and friends were more important than ever, and she was now determined to find joy in the everyday.

Which was why she'd agreed to accompany Ruby to the Autumnfest celebration this evening, instead of heading to New Windsor to examine a houseful of antiques before the items went to auction.

Josiah would always be with her, but just as she hoped he would get on with his life, she knew he would be hoping she would get on with hers.

This Friday outing would be a first step toward that goal. Sophie just wished the festival wasn't at the fairgrounds.

The bells over the door jingled, pulling Sophie's thoughts back to the present. A tall man with wavy blond hair that brushed his collar stepped into the store and glanced around.

The fact that her heart skittered, just a little, at the sight of him surprised her. Certainly, the guy was handsome, but she saw many good-looking guys, and none had caused such a reaction. Why him?

Sophie brushed aside the question and smiled. "Welcome to Timeless Treasures. Is there something I can help you find?"

Instead of pausing to look at any of the antiques lining the aisles, he headed straight to her, stopping in front of the counter.

"Good morning." He flashed a smile. "Are you Sophia Jessup?"

Something in the way he said *Sophia* had her heart tripping again. "I'm Sophie Jessup, the owner. How may I help you?"

"Joe Wexman." He extended his hand. "It's a pleasure to meet you."

His warm brown eyes were in sharp contrast to his blond hair. She liked how his smile was reflected in his eyes and the direct way he looked at her.

Josiah had looked at her like that, Sophie remembered. Her heart twisted.

"What can I do for you?" she asked again.

"You have my steamer trunk." For a second, he appeared uncertain. "Delanna Birch from Auction House said she spoke with you and that you were expecting me."

"Of course." Sophie gave a little laugh. "The Wexman name should have alerted me."

"I apologize for all this," he told her. "I don't know how the trunk and its contents got put in with the auction items. The fact that I didn't notice it had until Delanna called is on me."

"How so?" Without waiting for his response, she motioned for him to follow her into the back room.

"I was supposed to make sure all the items the family decided to keep remained separate from those we decided to auction off, but I'd just moved to GraceTown, and the semester was starting—" He stopped as if realizing he was rambling. "No need to bore you with my life story. The fact is, I fell down on the job, and I'm sorry to inconvenience you, but immensely grateful to have the trunk and its contents back."

"There it is." She swept a hand toward where the steamer trunk sat in the center of the room. "If you wait here, I'll go to the safe and get the money."

Confusion blanketed his handsome face. "What money?"

"The money that was in the trunk." She pulled together her brows. "I assumed that was the reason you responded in such a hurry to Delanna's call."

"There are things far more valuable to my family and me inside that trunk than any amount of cash."

Sophie chuckled. "Maybe. But this is a lot of money. Back in a sec."

When she returned with it, she found Joe had taken out the hatbox and opened the lid.

He lifted a hand holding a photograph as she approached. "These are what I meant. These photographs are family treasures. Aunt Mary offered to sort through them and put them in chronological order." A look of sadness crossed his face. "She became ill quite suddenly and passed away before she got the chance."

"I'm sorry for your loss." Sophie crouched down beside him. "Sudden losses can be devastating."

"Sounds as if you have some experience in that area."

Sophie simply nodded.

"I'm sorry for your loss, too."

"Yes, well, thank you." Sophie extended her hand. "Here's your cash."

His eyes widened. "Where did this come from?"

"It was in the trunk. My assistant and I had just started going through it when we stumbled across what he called a wad o' cash." Sophie shoved it into his hand when he didn't reach for it.

With obvious reluctance, he closed his fingers around the bills. "You could have kept this."

"It's not mine."

"You purchased the trunk."

"I did, but not the money someone hid inside it."

"Keep it," he said, his gaze returning to the hatbox. "This is what I want, what the family wants."

His entire face lit up when he spotted the velvet pouch. He immediately scooped it up.

"And this." He shook his head. "We thought this was gone forever. What's inside is, well, irreplaceable."

Sophie's heart stopped. Simply stopped beating. How could she tell him that she'd lost something that he and his family considered irreplaceable? Then again, how could she not?

She was still attempting to find her voice when he opened the drawstring.

"Mr. Wexman..." she began.

He didn't appear to hear her. Or, if he did, he was too intent on the contents of the pouch.

Sophie blinked when the love token fell into his hand.

Joe turned to her with a broad smile. "I don't know if you have ever seen one of these—"

"Wh-where did that come from?"

He smiled, continuing to turn the coin over and over in his fingers. "It was my Great-Great-Grandfather Josiah's"

Sophie stared at him. No way. Could it be?

"What was your great-great-grandfather's last name?" Sophie forced the words past her frozen lips.

"Huston. His name was Josiah Huston."

THAT EVENING, Sophie pulled her car into the parking lot of the fairgrounds to meet Ruby for Autumnfest. She'd barely turned off the ignition before her bestie stepped from her own vehicle and strode over.

"I'm so glad you agreed to come." Ruby gave her a quick hug the second she reached her. "I was starting to get worried about you."

Sophie gestured to the clear night sky with the yellow moon. "It's a beautiful evening."

The way Sophie saw it, if pretending all was well was what it took to get her family and friends to quit worrying about her, that's what she would do. "Joe Wexman stopped over this morning. He wasn't supposed to come until the weekend, but I looked up, and there he was."

"Was he excited about the money?" Ruby's dark eyes snapped with excitement.

"Not particularly." Sophie then gave her friend a blow-by-blow of that morning's encounter.

"That is unbelievable." Ruby shook her head. "Joe Wexman is Josiah's great-great-grandson. And the thing with the love token. You lose it at the fairgrounds, and somehow it ends up back in the trunk? That's positively creepy."

"It is strange." Sophie kept her tone light, though she preferred to think of it as unexplainable rather than creepy.

"Did he tell you how his family got the coin?"

"I didn't give him a chance." Sophie blew out a breath. "I acted like a crazy woman, Ruby. I told him there was something pressing that I forgot I needed to do. I said he could come back tomorrow and pick up the trunk, but for now I needed him to leave."

"What did he do?"

"He left." Sophie expelled a breath, recalling the confusion reflected in his brown depths.

"Did he leave the love token?"

"He took it with him."

"I can't wait to see him. You can bet I'll be there tomorrow when—" Ruby stopped in the middle of the walkway and made an exasperated sound.

"What's wrong?"

"Andrew is working tomorrow, not me."

"Stop in anyway. Mr. Wexman is coming by with a truck at ten."

"I can't. I have a hair appointment. Gemma is extremely difficult to get into, and if I cancel at the last minute, I'll probably be banned for life."

"I've heard of Gemma. Where is her salon located?"

"It's in her home. She lives in this huge old Victorian on Apple."

"I know the street. It's lovely." Apple Street was several blocks from Spruce Street, where Josiah lived. Gemma didn't live far at all from the home where Sophie and Josiah had danced in the living room.

Sophie had driven by Josiah's house shortly after the final incident at the fairgrounds. She hadn't stopped. There had been a moving van out front with men unloading furniture and boxes.

She and Ruby reached the front entrance, paid their five-dollar entry fee and stepped through the gate. A sign proclaiming "Pumpkin Nights and Fall Lights" in glittering letters sat in front of a display of carved pumpkins rising high into the air.

Ruby appeared in high spirits, chattering happily as they strode deeper into the fairgrounds.

With each step Sophie took down the festive main walkway, decorated with stalks of corn and colorful gourds, orange and yellow pumpkin lights strung overhead, she found herself seized with a feeling of impending doom.

Her heart began to race, and she broke out in a cold sweat.

Ruby's eyes brightened, and she waved wildly. "There's Mackenna."

Pressure began to build in Sophie's chest. She knew what was happening. She was on the verge of a full-fledged panic attack. "You know, Ruby, I'm feeling kind of funky. I think I'll head home."

"It's being at the fairgrounds again, isn't it?" Sympathy shone in Ruby's brown eyes. "I wondered if being here might be a problem."

"It's just been a busy week." Even as the pressure in her chest squeezed like a vise, Sophie reached over and touched Ruby's arm, wanting nothing more than to get away before she embarrassed them both. "I'll catch up with you this weekend."

Holding up a hand to the approaching Mackenna, Ruby turned to Sophie. "You wait here. I'll tell Mackenna we decided to do something else tonight. You and I can grab a coffee or a drink somewhere. Whatever sounds good to you."

"No." Sophie was already shaking her head before Ruby finished. "You hang with Mackenna. We'll touch base tomorrow."

"If you're sure?"

"I'm positive."

"Deal."

Sophie kept the smile on her face until Ruby reached Mackenna. She offered the women a smile and a wave, then turned down a quiet side path, where she hoped to find a spot to fall apart in private.

21

Choosing this path had been a good move, Sophie decided a moment later. Instead of swimming upstream against the people arriving at the fairgrounds, she found herself weaving between hay bales and stuffed scarecrows with pumpkin heads.

She was feeling steadier, until she passed a vendor wheeling a cotton candy machine toward the action. Sophie dropped down on a hay bale as tears slipped down her cheeks.

She thought the grief would become easier to bear, but it hadn't. The thought of what Josiah must have gone through, the pain he must have endured when she hadn't shown up that day still tore at her heart.

Her tears fell in a solid stream as sobs racked her body. She shouldn't have come here tonight. She wasn't ready. Wasn't sure if she would ever be ready.

"Are you okay?"

As if in a dream, she lifted her head. But it wasn't Josiah's warm blue eyes gazing at her with concern, it was Joe Wexman's brown ones.

Sophie felt the heat rise up her neck as she hurriedly swiped away the tears. It took a couple of seconds for her to find her voice. "I-I'm fine."

Joe gestured to the hay bale. "May I sit?"

The best she could offer was a little shrug. This was a community event. He could sit wherever he wanted. And she could get up and leave whenever she wanted.

"You look just like your picture, you know." His tone was conversational, though his eyes remained watchful.

She sniffled, wishing she had Josiah's handkerchief with her. The thought had the tears returning, but she determinedly blinked them back. "Picture?"

"Photograph. The one of you and Josiah in front of the Huston Ford GraceTown sign."

Sophie stilled.

"You're Sophia, the Sophie he spoke of, the woman who gave him a great gift—the ability to open his heart to another and love again."

"H-he spoke about me?"

Joe nodded. "That story has been passed down through the generations in my family."

"Why didn't you say something earlier today?" Sophie wasn't certain how Joe was so cool with the idea that time travel existed, but they could discuss that later. Right now, she needed to know all that had gone on in the days, months and years since she'd left. "Tell me something, did Josiah have a happy life?"

Please, please, please, say yes.

"He did." Joe offered a reassuring smile. "According to family lore, he waited for you to come as you'd agreed."

"I tried to come, but the love token got knocked out of my hand, and I couldn't find it. Then the tent was gone and—"

"He waited for you, and then he saw the love token on the ground, and he knew something had happened." Joe's eyes searched hers. "While his life was happy, he never forgot you and always prayed that you were happy in your time."

Sophie forced herself to breathe. In and out. In and out. "Tell me about his life after that day."

"About a year later, he married a woman his sister Edith—"

"I met Edith," Sophie interrupted. "She introduced Daisy, his first wife, to him."

"I didn't know that." Joe shared a smile with her, then continued. "Her name was Maybelle, and from everything I know, they had a long and happy life together. They had three sons and one daughter."

"Good. That's good." Sophie let out the breath she hadn't realized she'd been holding. "He wanted children."

"They named the girl Sophia."

Sophie closed her eyes as her heart swelled to be a sweet mass in her chest. "I'm so glad he was happy, that I didn't ruin things for him."

"You didn't." Joe reached over as if to squeeze her hand, then appeared to think better of it and let it drop. "From everything I know, you changed his life for the better."

Sophie gazed at him in confusion. "I know you said that stories have been passed down through the generations, but you seem so certain that he was happy. How do you know for sure? And how are you okay with the idea that time travel exists?"

"I'll start with the first question. Maybe it's the name."

She pulled her brows together.

"I'm also Josiah, though I've always gone by Joe. Maybe we're just a little more open to the unexplainable." Before she could say anything, he continued. "I'm also the family historian."

"If you're the family historian, why was the trunk containing so much of your family's history at Mary Wexman's home instead of your own?"

"Mary had been in that house for the last forty years. It was easier to keep the trunk there than to have it shipped to me." Joe's lips pressed together. "The steamer trunk getting added to the auction items was a huge mistake. I'm still trying to determine exactly how that happened."

"What about the money?"

"That, I can't explain, other than my great-aunt was known to frequent the casinos and became concerned about household staff stealing from her in her later years." Joe shrugged. "The only explanation my parents and I could come up with is that Mary hid the money in the trunk, then either forgot it was there or became too ill to retrieve it."

Sophie nodded, then asked, "How did you get to be the family historian?"

"My mother was before me." He smiled with fondness. "Once I finished my education, she passed all her knowledge down to me."

"And she told you about Josiah."

"Among other things." His expression turned solemn. "But there isn't a person in the family who didn't know the story about the woman who abruptly came into Josiah's life, then left just as abruptly, leaving him forever changed."

The knowledge that Josiah had experienced love again and had had a happy life soothed the raw spot in Sophie's heart. Though she wished desperately that she'd been the one to be with him, to love him for the rest of his life, to give him the children they both wanted, it was now apparent she'd been meant to come into his life for a season, not a lifetime.

Yet, if Joe was right, and she had made a difference, that would have to be enough.

"He changed me, too," Sophie heard herself say. "Because I knew him, I realized I don't have to settle. I believe I deserve a great love."

"I'm glad."

Sophie pushed to her feet. Her head spun, and her heart was both relieved and shredded at the same time. "I need to go."

Joe stood. "I can tell you more. If you want."

"I do want, but right now, I need to process."

"May I stop by and see how you're doing?"

When she opened her mouth to say...well, she wasn't certain what, he rushed ahead. "Josiah would want me to follow up."

Sophie nodded. He was right. That's exactly what Josiah would want.

"Okay. Sure. Stop by anytime." She began walking, and he fell into step beside her. Sophie slanted a glance at him. "You're leaving?"

"I'm walking you to your car." He smiled. "A safety thing."

Another thing Josiah would have done, except he would have extended his arm. Sophie could only nod as her heart began to ache.

When they reached her car, she turned back to him, having thought of one more question. "What is it you do, Joe?"

He rested his hand on the top of her car. "I'm a professor of folklore studies at Collister College."

Joe arrived the next morning in a pickup. The steamer trunk, with Sophie's and Andrew's assistance, was hefted into the back of the truck. Sophie had her emotions firmly under control, but when Joe asked if she'd like to grab a coffee, she'd told him she was working today.

An hour later, he returned to drop off a latte and a scone, thanking her again for taking such good care of the trunk. Once again, he tried to give her the money that had been in the trunk, but she refused.

She gave him a little wave and a smile when he left the store, the photograph he'd given her, the one of her with Josiah taken that day in the showroom, clutched in her fingers.

"Was that Joe Wexman?" Ruby asked as she strode into the shop only minutes later.

"He dropped off a latte and scone as a kind of thank-you," Sophie told her friend, then lifted the photograph. "And he gave me this."

Ruby's eyes widened. Her gaze shifted between the picture and Sophie. "Wow, that is an amazing picture. You and Josiah look so happy together."

"It means the world to me." Sophie lifted the mocha latte and absently took a sip.

"Are you going to be seeing Joe again?" Ruby asked, breaking off a piece of orange scone and popping it into her mouth.

"He said he'd keep checking in, in case I have more questions." Sophie paused. "I probably will, but the information he gave me, that Josiah had a happy life, is what I really wanted to know."

"Maybe you and Joe could, I don't know, go out sometime." At Sophie's disbelieving look, Ruby shrugged. "You have a lot in common."

"I'm not ready for any of that." Still, as Sophie took another sip of her latte, she realized that for the first time since the coin had spurted from her hand, she could breathe easy again.

Over the next months, Joe continued to stop by Timeless Treasures. Only he started staying longer and longer, as they would get to talking about all sorts of things. Her feelings for him grew and the hole in her heart, the one she thought would never be filled, began to close.

In early November, he paused at the door and turned back to

her, his expression suddenly serious. He cleared his throat. "Sophie, I believe people show up in our lives for a reason. There was a reason you came into Josiah's life, and now there's a reason you've come into mine. How about we go find out what it is?"

EPILOGUE

O*ne year later*

By Christmas, Joe had met her family.

By the time the leaves started returning to the trees and the air turned warm, they were inseparable. How he made her feel, her connection to him, might be different from what she shared with Josiah, but it was just as powerful.

On a lovely Friday in May, Joe asked her to marry him, and she said yes.

Now, today, they were gathered in the parlor of Joe's home on Spruce, the same parlor where she'd danced the Bunny Hug with Josiah, surrounded by family and friends to say their vows. The sparkling emerald-cut diamond on her left hand winked in the glow of the candles.

Joe's brown eyes overflowed with love as he spoke his vows. "Sophia Jessup, I feel incredibly lucky to be standing here beside you, promising my love. I believe we were always meant to be together. Sometimes people come into our lives for a season and others for a lifetime. You are my forever love. I promise that I will love you and honor you every day for the rest of our lives."

Sophie blinked back tears of joy that sprang to her eyes, and she thought of the love token resting in a special pocket of her ivory gown. *Love Be Yours, Love Be Mine.*

"My love is yours, Josiah Wexman," Sophie murmured as she began her vows, "not just for a season, but for a lifetime."

I HOPE you enjoyed reading The Love Token as much as I loved writing it! I have to admit the GraceTown series is a favorite of mine and I know you are going to adore the next book in the series, The Angel in the Square. Even though each book can standalone, you will see friends from The Pink House and The Love Token in this uplifting story that will keep you reading waaay too late at night!

In 1919, when doors were locked and windows were shuttered against disease, an angel came to GraceTown. She moved from

house to house, nursing the sick and breathing life into the community—and then she disappeared. The only evidence of her existence a stone angel in her likeness in the town square...

Nurse Jenna Woodsen doesn't know anything about the Angel of GraceTown or the statue honoring her in the community's town square.

She only knows that when she and her elderly aunt were forced to flee Philadelphia in the dead of night, Violet--the wayward traveler Jenna picked up--suggested they shelter in a deserted house in GraceTown.

Violet, a doppelganger for the angel in the square, insists they will be safe here. Everyone assumes Jenna is the fiancée of the absentee homeowner and Violet convinces Jenna to play along.

Jenna is slowly rebuilding her interrupted life when her "fiancé" shows up. Will Daniel's arrival cause Jenna and her aunt to run again? Or is his appearance part of a bigger plan that will allow Jenna to face her past and fully embrace the life she's found in GraceTown?

Rich in plot, emotions, and characters, this is a book you won't soon forget. So, sit back, prop up your feet and take a break from reality today!

Order your copy now or keep reading for a sneak peek:

SNEAK PEEK OF THE ANGEL IN THE SQUARE

Chapter 1

Balancing the cake box in one hand, Jenna Woodsen used the other to ring the bell of the nondescript house on Philadelphia's north side. Even though working here as a house parent could be challenging, Jenna would miss her weekend shifts.

The door flung open, and Keisha, a tall woman with an explosion of black curls and bright red lipstick, motioned her inside. "Sorry to keep you waiting. I dropped a plate in the kitchen and was cleaning up the mess."

"No problem." Though the rain was more of a heavy mist, not uncommon for April, the porch roof had allowed Jenna to stay dry while she waited. "Can I help?"

"All done." Once Jenna was inside, Keisha shut the door, then flipped the deadbolt.

Jenna glanced around. "Where are the girls?"

Last weekend, there had been six, all between the ages of 13 and 17. The number who lived here constantly fluctuated. Sometimes, because a girl was reunited with her family or because the caseworker had found a foster home willing to take one of the teens. And, rarely, it was because one of the girls aged out of the system.

"Misty and Denisha are in their rooms. Jubilee, Suri and Ella are in the living room. Violet—"

"—is right here." Violet, tall and slender with a mass of strawberry-blond curls and large blue eyes, smiled at Jenna. "You came."

Pleasure ran through the girl's words like a pretty ribbon.

"I told you I would." Jenna held out the bakery box. "What's an eighteenth birthday without a cake?"

Violet's blue eyes never left Jenna's face. "Letting you go isn't fair."

Jenna shot a quick glance at Keisha.

The woman immediately raised her hands. "Don't look at me. I didn't say nothing to nobody. I figured I'd leave that up to you."

Shifting her gaze back to Violet, Jenna cocked her head. "Do the others know?"

"Not yet."

"How did you hear?"

Violet lifted one thin shoulder, then let it drop. "Does it matter?"

Keisha chuckled. "The girl has a point."

Jenna let it go. How Violet had heard didn't matter. After tonight's birthday celebration, Jenna would tell the rest of the girls that her part-time position had been eliminated.

She could have let them figure it out when there was only one staff member on duty this weekend, not two. But she'd forged a bond with them, and they'd already experienced enough friends and family walking away without a backward glance.

Jenna's gaze slid from Keisha to Violet. "Is this a good time for cake?"

"The way I figure, it's always a good time for cake." Keisha chuckled and glanced at Violet. "How about you, birthday girl? Are you ready to get this party started?"

Violet grinned. "I am."

The two followed Jenna into the kitchen. They watched her take brightly colored party plates and plastic forks from a bag she'd brought with her before lifting the cake from the box.

"Incredible." Violet stared, wide-eyed, at the gorgeous confection that boasted a star charm rising above the cake on a swirl of LED lights.

"You're a rising star, Violet." Jenna's voice filled with emotion. "In my heart, I know you're destined to do big things."

"Thank you, Jenna." A soft look stole over Violet's face. "Not only for the amazing cake, but for the support you've given me."

Impulsively, Jenna gave her a quick hug. "Happy, happy birthday, sweet Violet."

When Jenna stepped back, she found Keisha staring.

Jenna raised a hand to her cheek. "Do I have something on my face?"

Keisha shook her head and smiled. "It's just when I see the two of you together, I can't get over how much you look alike."

This wasn't the first time someone had made that observation. Though their hair and eye colors were different, Jenna had to admit her facial features and Violet's were very similar.

"Of course we look alike." Violet shot Jenna a wink. "She's my big sis."

Jenna chuckled. Instead of going by the traditional "house parent" moniker, staff members at this group home were referred to as "big sisters."

An hour later, after the singing, candle-blowing and everyone enjoying delicious cake from one of the finest bakeries in Philadelphia, it was time for Jenna to leave.

Keisha had to make sure everyone's chores were done and

that the girls were ready for school tomorrow. Everyone except for Violet, who'd graduated midterm.

The only thing left was for Jenna to let the other girls know she wouldn't be coming back. Most acted like they didn't care. Jenna knew differently.

After saying good-bye to each of them, Jenna turned to Violet. "Walk me to the door?"

She soon stood alone in the entryway, facing the tall girl on the brink of womanhood. A face full of freckles made her appear younger, but her eyes, deep and knowing, said she'd already seen more than most.

"You'll soon be on your own." Jenna met Violet's gaze. "I want you to remember that you're strong and smart and capable of doing whatever you set your mind to. I firmly believe your future holds much happiness."

Violet settled a hand on Jenna's shoulder and met her gaze. "I believe yours holds the same."

"You've got my number. If there's ever anything I can do for you—"

"I'm certain our paths will cross again." Without warning, Violet wrapped her arms around Jenna and squeezed tight. "For now, take care of you."

~

On the drive home that night, Jenna pondered Violet's words and wondered if her worry over the loss of the part-time income had shown.

Jenna was the sole support for herself and her great-aunt Rosemary, so the money she'd earned at the group home had been a buffer for the unexpected. Her full-time position as an RN caregiver for Cherise Menard covered their regular expenses, but Jenna had liked the cushion.

The next few days passed quickly. On Friday, when Jenna arrived at her day job, it struck her that once this shift ended, she had the entire weekend free. Perhaps she and Rosemary could go to the Philadelphia Museum of Art tomorrow. Or maybe visit the nearby Amish country and pick up some Dutch apple jam or a shoefly pie.

Throughout the day while caring for Cherise, Jenna happily considered the options. After giving the day's report to Timothy, who would cover the evening shift, Jenna was nearly to the door when Britta, the housekeeper and one of Jenna's good friends, called her name.

She turned, surprised when the petite brunette hurried over to her. "Mr. Menard wants to speak with you."

Although Michael Menard had been the one to initially interview and hire her, she'd had little contact with him since.

That had been fine with Jenna. While she genuinely enjoyed Cherise, there was something about the woman's husband that she found off-putting. He was arrogant, which she expected from someone in his position, but it was the hint of mean in his eyes that had her keeping her distance.

Not that he'd ever sought her out. Until now.

Britta gestured. "He's in the study."

Jenna knocked on the open door, and he motioned her inside.

"Close the door," he ordered in a brusque tone.

Her heart tripped, and she clasped her hands together to still their trembling. She told herself she had nothing to worry about. Cherise liked her, and Mr. Menard could have no complaints about the quality of the care she gave his wife.

Dressed in one of his expensive suits, with his short hair holding just enough gray to give off a distinguished vibe, Michael Menard was the picture of a successful businessman.

With a hand sporting perfectly manicured nails, he gestured her to a leather visitor's chair. "Have a seat."

Once she did, instead of sitting behind the ornate executive desk as he had when he interviewed her, he sat on the edge of the desk. He was so close she could smell the not-so-subtle scent of his cologne.

It was a popular fragrance, an expensive one, but not one she liked. Right now, the smell of it had her stomach lurching.

When he said nothing, Jenna offered a bright smile. "Britta said you wanted to see me."

He appeared puzzled, then he waved a dismissive hand. "Ah, yes, the housekeeper."

Falling silent, he appraised her with cool blue eyes.

Jenna shifted in her scrubs, which were a soft raspberry. As Cherise didn't want to feel as if she were in a hospital or health center, her caregivers were instructed to wear high-end scrubs in any color except white or gray.

When Jenna had left the house, Rosemary had told her today's scrubs color made her eyes look like pools of melted chocolate. The comment had made her smile.

Right now, she didn't feel like smiling. Something in Mr. Menard's gaze had her shifting uneasily in her seat.

"Cherise told me you lost your second job." A look of sympathy crossed his face. "That has to be quite a blow. I'm sure you count on the extra income."

Normally, Jenna wouldn't have mentioned the loss of the group-home position to Cherise, but the woman, a former civic activist, loved listening to Jenna's stories about the girls. Of course, Jenna always carefully omitted names and any identifying personal information.

When Cherise had asked about the girls earlier in the week, Jenna had felt obligated to tell her what had happened.

Never in a million years had she thought that Cherise would

bring the situation up to her husband. Or that he'd be interested enough to mention it.

"Budget cuts." Jenna offered what she hoped looked like an unconcerned shrug. "It happens."

"Still, you don't have a husband or boyfriend to fall back on."

Despite finding the comment with the underlying question a bit personal, Jenna told herself the man was only showing concern. "No. No husband or boyfriend. Just me and my great-aunt, Rosemary."

The man's lips lifted ever so slightly. "That's what I thought. Cherise has mentioned your aunt, too. Must be quite the burden, having her depend on you for everything."

"My great-aunt is not a burden." Jenna fought to keep the offense from her voice.

"Of course not. I simply meant that it must be hard, financially speaking. Especially now."

"I appreciate your concern, but Rosemary is waiting for me." With great effort, Jenna resisted glancing at the door. "If that's all—"

"I like you, Jenna. You seem like a bright girl. You clearly care about your aunt and," his eyes scanned her body, "yourself. I get the impression ensuring your aunt's well-being is important to you. Am I right?"

Jenna nodded. "That's right."

"Good. Because I have a way for you to earn extra cash. It's not something I'd offer to just anyone." He leaned closer to her and dropped his voice to a conspiratorial whisper. "Plus, I think it's the kind of thing a girl like you will like." He offered her a smile that reminded her of one she'd seen last year in his campaign ads, then named a figure. "Interested?"

Jenna's wariness was replaced by excitement. "Yes. I mean, possibly. What would it involve?"

Her smile fell away as he told her in explicit terms what she would be doing to earn that money.

Bile rose in her throat as she pushed back her chair and stood. "I'm not interested." But when she turned toward the door, his hand closed around her wrist in a steely grip.

"Not so fast."

Before she knew what was happening, he jerked her against him. "Let me give you a sample of what you'd be missing."

With one hand still locked around her wrist, his free arm snaked around her like a vise as he crushed his mouth against hers.

She struggled, but he had a good hundred pounds on her and a tight grip.

When he finally released his hold on her wrist to squeeze her breast, Jenna seized the moment. Grabbing the first item she could lay a hand on, a paperweight on the desk, she slammed it against the side of his head.

He stumbled back, raising his hand to his temple. When he lowered it and saw the blood, he let out a roar. "You goddamn bitch."

Jenna didn't wait to hear more and fled.

Wade Spahr, Mr. Menard's assistant, stood in the foyer, talking on his cellphone. He glanced up in mild annoyance as she rushed past.

Once out of the house, Jenna sprinted to her car, jerked open the door and jumped inside. She locked the doors before peeling off in the direction of home.

The apartment building where she lived was in sight when her phone rang. Jenna pulled into her parking spot and glanced at the screen. *Britta.*

"Hello." Jenna's voice shook. No surprise, as the rest of her body currently had the shakes.

"Jenna. I need to warn you—"

"If it's about Mr. Menard being a perv, I already know."

"It's worse than that. Mr. Menard is saying you assaulted him."

"I didn't assault him! He's the one who assaulted *me*. I hit him in self-defense." The tears Jenna had held in check all the way home slipped down her cheeks. "If I hadn't gotten away, I think he would have..."

Jenna's voice thickened, the realization of what she'd narrowly escaped hitting her full force.

"Oh, Jenna..."

"It's over." Taking a deep breath, Jenna let it out slowly and felt herself steady. "I'm going to speak with the agency and let them know what happened. I can't go back."

When Britta said nothing, Jenna added, "No matter how much I like Cherise, I can't work in that house, Britta. Not with him there."

"There's more, Jenna." Britta hesitated. "After you left, I overheard him talking to Mr. Spahr. The door was shut, but he was so angry he was practically screaming. Mr. Menard plans to pin the thefts on you. He's going to say that he walked in on you taking the jewels from the safe in his office and that you struck him when he tried to detain you. Mr. Spahr will back him up."

Jenna brought a hand to her head, which had started to spin. "Are you talking about Cherise's jewels?"

"Yes."

Several months earlier, Cherise had reported to police that over a hundred thousand dollars' worth of family jewels had been stolen. Thankfully, the rest of the gems had been locked away in the safe in her husband's office.

"If they charge you, it will be a felony."

"I didn't take anything." Jenna's voice rose, then cracked.

"I know you didn't. You know you didn't. But who will the police believe? Especially if Mr. Spahr corroborates what Mr. Menard said and says they caught you in the act." Britta's voice held a warning edge. "I heard him call the police and request an officer be sent over."

"I didn't take any jewelry," Jenna repeated. "He assaulted me. The only way I could get away was to hit him with that paperweight."

"It will be his word against yours. Even if I tell them what I overheard, Mr. Menard will say you and I friends, and I'm just covering for you." Resignation filled Britta's voice. "Who do you think the police will believe? The important city councilmember? Or you?"

"I can't believe you took a sabbatical from work so we could take a road trip." Rosemary, a handsome woman with deep-set blue eyes and a gray braid hanging down her back, gave a happy sigh. "Just taking off in a car and driving with no particular destination in mind reminds me of my youthful adventures."

Jenna slanted a smile at her great-aunt. "It'll be fun."

Once she'd gotten her emotions under control, Jenna had considered how to spin getting the heck out of Dodge, er, Philadelphia. The last thing she wanted was to worry her great-aunt. Rosemary had a weak heart, and doctors had advised Jenna to help her avoid stress, not bring it home to her.

Rosemary wasn't easily fooled, but she'd believed Jenna when she'd said she'd been saving money from her second job so they could have this vacation. And she hadn't blinked an eye when Jenna told her to make sure she took whatever she wouldn't want to leave behind in case they found the perfect spot and didn't want to leave.

The six months of living expenses that Jenna had set aside for a rainy day had been withdrawn from the bank. If the possibility of being charged with a second-degree felony punishable by ten years in prison and a twenty-five-thousand-dollar fine didn't qualify as a rainy day, Jenna didn't know what would.

When Rosemary had brought up Cherise, Jenna's heart had given a little ping. She'd assured her aunt that the Menards could get by just fine without her.

Wanting to get as far away from Philadelphia as quickly as possible, Jenna took Washington Avenue on her way to I-95. She slowed to stop at a light. That's when she saw her.

The thin girl, carrying a duffel with a cross-body strap, wore a hoodie that was no match for today's brisk wind.

Jenna pointed, her tone reflecting her shock. "That girl on the sidewalk is Violet."

"Violet from the group home?"

"Yes."

While they watched, Violet moved close to the curb and stuck a thumb in the air.

Jenna frowned. "She's hitchhiking."

"That's a dangerous thing to do these days." Concern filled Rosemary's voice.

At any other time, Jenna would have immediately pulled over and picked her up. But did she really want to draw Violet into the mess that was her life right now? If the police stopped them, could Violet be charged with aiding a criminal simply for being in the car?

Rosemary touched Jenna's arm. "You can't allow a stranger to pick her up," she said urgently.

No, Jenna thought, she couldn't. Ignoring the blare of horns, Jenna wheeled the car across traffic and stopped at the side of the road.

Jenna lowered the window on Rosemary's side and leaned across her aunt as Violet stepped to the side of the car.

"What are you doing hitchhiking?" Fear had the question coming out sharper than Jenna had intended.

"Why are you running away?" Violet responded mildly.

"We're not running," Rosemary answered before Jenna could. "We're off on an adventure. Please get in. Wherever you're headed, we'll take you there."

"That's a generous offer," Violet said as she slid into the back seat, tossing her duffel to one side and fastening her seat belt, "considering you don't even know where I'm going."

"Doesn't matter."

Violet returned Rosemary's smile. "I'm headed to Grace-Town, Maryland."

Jenna pulled her brows together. "Is that near Baltimore?"

"About fifty miles west."

"Why there?" Jenna asked, pulling back into traffic.

In the rearview mirror, she saw Violet shrug. "I spent some time there years ago. It's time to go back."

Rosemary smiled. "Jenna and I are going wherever the wind takes us. It sounds as if GraceTown will be our first stop."

"If you need a place to crash once we get there, I know of a house that's empty." Violet covered a yawn with her fingers. "Save you money on a motel."

Beside Jenna, her aunt's eyes lit up. "It's been a long time since I crashed anywhere."

Jenna thought of the money she'd taken out of her savings account that morning. Money that would go a lot further if they didn't have to pay for housing for a night or two.

"The place has been vacant for years," Violet added, obviously sensing Jenna's hesitation.

"How do you know this?"

"I know a lot of things." Violet chuckled. "Like, didn't I tell you we'd meet again?"

ALSO BY CINDY KIRK

Good Hope Series

The Good Hope series is a must-read for those who love stories that uplift and bring a smile to your face.

GraceTown Series

Enchanting stories that are a perfect mixture of romance, friendship, and magical moments set in a community known for unexplainable happenings.

Hazel Green Series

These heartwarming stories, set in the tight-knit community of Hazel Green, are sure to move you, uplift you, inspire and delight you. Enjoy uplifting romances that will keep you turning the page!

Holly Pointe Series

Readers say "If you are looking for a festive, romantic read this Christmas, these are the books for you."

Jackson Hole Series

Heartwarming and uplifting stories set in beautiful Jackson Hole, Wyoming.

Silver Creek Series

Engaging and heartfelt romances centered around two powerful families whose fortunes were forged in the Colorado silver mines.

Sweet River Montana Series

A community serving up a slice of small-town Montana life, where helping hands abound and people fall in love in the context of home and family.